THE LONG SHADOW OF DEATH

Book 3 in *The Long Shadow* Thriller Series

Nichole Heydenburg

The Long Shadow of Death
Copyright © 2022 by Poisoned Ink Press LLC

All Rights Reserved. No part of this book may be used or reproduced in any manner whatsoever without written permission except in the case of brief quotations embodied in critical articles or reviews.

Contact Information: www.nicholeheydenburg.com
poisonedinkpress@gmail.com

Cover Design: Stone Ridge Books

ISBN 978-1-7349015-4-2 (eBook)
ISBN 978-1-7349015-5-9 (paperback)

This book is a work of fiction. All characters, incidents, names, and places are utilized fictitiously or are the product of the author's imagination. Any similarity to real persons, living or dead, events, or businesses is completely coincidental.

Dedicated to Alex

For always believing in me, for helping me bring this series to life,
and for our friendship that will last a lifetime.

The Long Shadow of Death

Other Books by Nichole Heydenburg

The Long Shadow on the Stage- Book 1 in *The Long Shadow Thriller Series*

The Long Shadow of Memory- Book 2 in *The Long Shadow Thriller Series*

Prologue

August 2016

Blood poured down Edgar's face and blurred his vision. He squinted through the blood and tried to see his attacker. He had to find a way to fight back. He needed to survive. After all he had been through, this couldn't be the end. The next bullet hit Edgar on the right side of his chest, making him scream. The pain was overwhelming. He could barely force himself to move, as he crawled away, leaving a trail of bloody splatters behind him. The third bullet struck next to the second one and also buried itself in Edgar's chest.

Edgar gasped for breath and clutched at his chest, as he saw the blood soaking his T-shirt. He knew this was it.

Chapter 1: Edgar

Three Months after the Arrest- July 2016

Edgar paced the cell, muttering to himself in the 10-foot-by-10-foot, enclosed space which comprised white cinderblock walls, a bed with a lumpy mattress and thin blanket, and a metal toilet. He recalled the fear he felt when he was threatened by an inmate on his first day in prison. He had been moved to his own cell because the guards and the Minneapolis Police Department were concerned about what would happen to Edgar if he was left around the other inmates unsupervised. It was July, one of the nicest months in Minnesota, but unfortunately for Edgar, he wasn't able to enjoy much of the warm weather. Several months had passed since Delia, Jerry, and the Minneapolis Police Department found him at his parents' house and arrested him for the murders. The funny thing was no one knew how many people he killed and Edgar was sure they would never find the bodies of Liam or his dad. The police found his mom's body, freshly killed, lying on the kitchen floor in her house. If they had arrived sooner, they probably could have saved her, but they wasted their time banging on the door and waiting for Edgar to let them in before they finally picked the lock. The thought made Edgar smirk. There was also the matter of Jackson's and Clara's deaths, but no one had been able to prove Edgar killed them, due to lack of evidence, lazy policework, and negligent police officers and detectives. Edgar wasn't sure what was going to happen to him, but he knew he was in a tough situation now. He needed to find a way out of prison. He needed a plan.

While he awaited his trial, he was being held at the Harriet Heights Maximum Security Prison, the highest security prison in Minnesota. A camera followed him as he paced his cell and there was a rotating shift of guards stationed outside of his cell. He was allowed to leave the cell for an hour of exercise each day in the tiny prison yard, where he was accompanied by two guards. He avoided interacting with the other inmates because he didn't want to associate with their kind. Pedophiles, rapists, and serial killers. He wasn't like them and didn't want to become wrapped up in any trouble while he was in prison. The lack of human contact for months was enough to drive an ordinary person mad, but Edgar had been mad for some time now.

Edgar continued his pacing, eyeing the current guard stationed outside of his cell, who had a thin mustache and a buzzcut and leaned against the wall opposite the cell, dozing on and off. As Edgar contemplated his existence that was beginning to feel more and more futile, a figure fizzled into existence on his bed.

"I was wondering when you were going to show up again," Edgar said quietly, glancing at the guard to make sure he couldn't hear him. He didn't need to look directly at the shadowy figure to know who it was. He was used to his former best friend's unexplainable appearances by now.

The guard was still dozing and hadn't noticed the other presence in the cell yet.

The former human who perched on the edge of the bed had been handsome once, attractive enough for millions of people around the world to fall in love with him week after week on the popular detective show, *Dispatching David*. Now, his dark hair was crusted over with blood, his formerly bright green eyes appeared dull and hollow, and his smile was more eerie than charming. But the aspects of his appearance that made him almost unrecognizable were the hole in his head that a bullet had traveled through, his hair crumbled with flecks of blood and flesh, his decaying frame, and the smell that emanated from the figure that threatened to make Edgar vomit every time he appeared, even more so in the small, enclosed space.

"Hello, Edgar," he said, the corners of his lips turning up into what some might call a smile.

Edgar squinted and adjusted his glasses, which he had started wearing again after his arrest. "What do you want, Jackson?"

Jackson smirked, stretching his arms widely. "Not much space to breathe in here, is there?"

Edgar rolled his eyes. "Are you here to make me feel worse about being stuck in prison? Because if you are, you can leave now."

Jackson halted his stretching and leaned back on the bed, resting against the wall and staring directly at Edgar. "No, I'm here to help."

Edgar raised an eyebrow. "How do you plan on doing that?"

"I'm going to get you out of here."

Edgar took a step away from the bed, wrinkling his nose in disgust. "I really wish you could do something about that smell."

Jackson chuckled and shook his head. "The smell is all in your head, Edgar. You can stop it whenever you want. You realize you're facing life in prison, right? Escaping is your only way to freedom."

Edgar shook his head vigorously, as if trying to make Jackson disappear. "Stop it! You're not here. You're not real," he screamed.

The guard stationed in the hall across from his cell jerked awake and sprang over to the cell. "Hey! What's going on?"

Edgar looked at the guard and froze momentarily as he realized his predicament.

The guard's formerly drowsy expression became menacing as he banged on the door of the cell. "I asked you a question, scum."

Edgar glanced at the bed surreptitiously, noting that Jackson was gone and sighed in relief. He ignored the guard, doing his best to remain calm and not antagonize the guard.

"Are you ignoring me?" The guard scrunched up his face in anger and he rummaged around his belt for the key card to the cell.

Edgar stepped back as far as he could in the cell, so that he was against the far wall, as his heart pounded loud enough to wake the dead.

The guard found the key card and unlocked the door, took several long strides toward Edgar and roughly grabbed his arms, then handcuffed his hands together.

Edgar had remained on his best behavior and kept a low profile the last few months. He was intent on leaving prison and didn't want to be punished for breaking the rules.

"You're going to solitary confinement for a week for disrespecting me. We don't tolerate that type of attitude in here. Maybe a week by yourself will straighten you out and make you think twice before disrespecting me like that again," the guard said nastily, spit flying from his mouth as he pulled Edgar out of the cell and shut the door.

"But I'm already in a cell by myself. And I didn't do anything!" Edgar protested.

"Solitary confinement is much worse than the luxurious place you've been staying, asshole."

The guard pulled Edgar down the hallway to the solitary confinement cell. It was an even smaller space, but the room was completely absent of light and there weren't any windows. Even the door was part of the solid wall, which ensured anyone in solitary confinement was alone, with nothing to look at or distract them, left to their own thoughts. Apparently, he wasn't going to double check with the prison warden or ask permission to put Edgar in solitary.

The guard unlocked the door and shoved Edgar inside. "See ya in a week, buddy," he said, chuckling as he locked the door. He whistled as he walked away.

Edgar slumped down onto the floor in the darkness. He had never felt so alone. He pondered the events that led him to this point. He could trace back the blame for his almost certain conviction, his arrest, and all the other terrible things that happened to him over the last year. It all led back to the same person and the thought of her infuriated him because she had caught him in the end, despite his best efforts.

Many inmates had tried over the years, but no one escaped the Harriet Heights Maximum Security Prison. Edgar planned to be the first one to break out, and when he did, he was going straight for that bitch Delia to get his revenge.

8

Chapter 2: Delia

The past few months, Delia had been forced to deal with being somewhat of a celebrity. After she was involved in Edgar's arrest, her name and photo were plastered across every major newspaper, online articles, ABC7 New York, NBC New York, and FOX 5 New York. She hadn't expected it to happen and wished she could go back to her previous life of being an unknown entity, invisible, in a city full of millions of people.

Delia sat cross-legged on the futon in her temporary bedroom, trying to concentrate on reading a book she recently purchased from The Strand Book Store in NYC. She claimed it was her temporary residence, but three months had passed since she moved into Becca and Joel's house and brought her puggle, Lily, with her. The room was decently sized: the walls were painted a light gray with a slight shimmer, the carpet was a tannish color, the futon was currently folded upright into the couch position against one wall, the other wall had a small, antique white desk against it with a wooden chair in front of it that looked so fragile Delia was scared to sit in it. Delia stared at her laptop on the desk charging, with a few notebooks and assorted pens next to it. There were two windows in front of the desk, each with sheer, gray drapes covering them. She usually kept the drapes closed. The windows looked out onto an alleyway where there were several parked cars and trash cans. Not exactly a picturesque, inspiring view.

Delia tossed the book aside wearily without bothering to place a bookmark in it to mark her page. She couldn't concentrate on reading. She couldn't remember the last time she slept more than a few hours and reading required a mental capacity that she didn't currently have. Besides, she didn't usually read, unless it was police reports or information and research pertaining to an investigation. The only exception was that she read any books published by her best friend, Becca, who was a moderately successful murder mystery writer.

She reached for her phone on the nightstand next to the futon to check the time. 9:55 a.m. She set her phone back down and idly opened the single drawer of the nightstand, which housed Delia's gun and ammunition. She shut the drawer again after confirming her gun was still safely inside.

Delia stood from the futon and walked across the room, where the closet was full. Most of Delia's clothes were hanging in the closet or shoved into suitcases, with her shoes, weapons, and other necessary investigative gear stacked haphazardly on the floor of the closet. She pulled a shirt and jeans from one of her suitcases and put on the clothes.

Several pictures Becca and Joel photographed on their various trips around the world hung on the walls in handcrafted, wooden frames that Joel made. Lily's plush dog bed was placed next to the futon and she laid in it, lazily staring at Delia from the other side of the room. Overall, it was a pleasant room if you were a guest staying a few nights, but Delia was suffocating, with only the room to retreat to when she needed alone time. She was used to living by herself and accustomed to not worrying about sharing a living space, not to mention sharing the single full-sized bathroom with two other people.

Delia sold and donated as many of her belongings as possible before she moved in with Becca and Joel because their 1,200 square foot fixer-upper in Queens didn't have much room to store her unnecessary items. Unfortunately, Delia still had to pay for a storage unit, which contained her favorite pieces of furniture, possessions of her mom's that she couldn't bear to part with, and her immense teacup collection.

Delia glanced at her phone again. It was still only 10:00 a.m. She was supposed to be eating brunch with Becca and Joel in their dining room at 11:00 a.m., but she didn't want to leave the room too early. She suspected the topic of their thinly masqueraded brunch invitation and dreaded the conversation. She was thankful they took her in when she impulsively quit her job, ran through most of her savings, and could no longer afford her apartment in NYC. They had been her closest friends since high school. After her mom and her friend Jerry both unexpectedly died in the spring, Becca and Joel were two of the only people left in the world that she loved. Unless you counted Lily, of course, because Delia loved her as much as a person can love an animal companion.

As Delia contemplated all the loss she recently endured, she finally accepted that her mom's Alzheimer's and the strokes she suffered that ultimately resulted in her death weren't her fault. There was nothing she could have done to stop her mom from dying. That didn't make it much easier to deal with, but she tried her best to cope with the loss and forgive herself for not spending as much time with her mom as she should have when her health began to deteriorate. However, Jerry's death was different. It could have been prevented. He didn't need to die. If she hadn't dragged Jerry into helping her with the Jackson Birkman case, the one she had been obsessed with, then he would still be alive. It was her fault Edgar killed him.

Chapter 3: Edgar

Edgar arrived at Jackson and Clara's apartment for a movie night. He walked down the hallway to the family room, where Jackson's 60-inch TV hung proudly on the wall, flanked on either side by shelves filled with DVDs and video games. No one was sitting on the worn leather couch he helped Jackson pick out back when they were recent college grads and Jackson was furnishing his first apartment.

"Jackson?" he called out tentatively, as he headed toward the kitchen.

Where are they? he wondered as he paused in the kitchen, horrified at what he saw. Blood splatters covered the once pristine white tile floors. His mom's body was splayed out near the stove, a bloodied kitchen knife next to her. Edgar took a step back and covered his mouth, not daring to move any closer to his mom because she was clearly dead.

Edgar exited the kitchen and entered the master bedroom, which was at the end of the hallway. Edgar smelled the decay before he entered the room and prepared himself for what he was about to see. Jackson and Clara both laid lifeless on the king-sized bed, with identical gunshot wounds in their heads. As Edgar inched closer to their bodies, Jackson's body started to decay rapidly as if he had pressed fast forward during a scene in a horror movie. Flesh fell off in chunks onto the satin duvet covering the bed. Edgar covered his mouth and tried to quell the urge to vomit. He closed his eyes for a moment, attempting to calm himself.

When Edgar slowly opened his eyes again, praying that the bodies would be gone and that he imagined the whole thing, he screamed at what he now saw on the bed. Jackson sat up, leaning against the headboard, his lifeless eyes staring at him. When Jackson noticed Edgar looking at him, he smiled, his mouth curling into the most unpleasant grin Edgar had seen on Jackson's formerly handsome face.

"You can't get rid of us, Edgar. I'll never let you forget what you did to me," Jackson said menacingly.

Jackson stood from the bed and Edgar expected Jackson to walk toward him. Instead, Jackson hovered several inches above the ground and floated in his direction, leaving a trail of rotting flesh on the carpet as he moved. Edgar stared, not moving, not believing what was happening. The closer Jackson moved to Edgar, the more overwhelming the stench became, until Edgar couldn't handle it anymore. Jackson's face was only inches away from his, the smell nearly suffocating him, when Jackson leaned in until their faces were practically touching—

Edgar woke, screaming over and over. He couldn't stop the frightened cries erupting from his mouth, couldn't shake the terrible image of Jackson's dead body coming to life and the smell that emanated from his best friend. He knew it was his fault Jackson was dead, but he hadn't expected to still be haunted by his actions months after the murder. He didn't feel any guilt over Clara's death. She deserved what happened to her. She never loved Jackson the way he did.

As far as his mom, he didn't regret killing her either. He only wished he knew her better before she threatened to betray him. She would have taken him down with her if he hadn't killed her. It was for the best, but who knew how many secrets she took with her to the grave? Edgar would never know the truth about how his dad died. Or if his younger brother's death was really an accident as his mom claimed.

Edgar wondered when the nightmares would stop and if Jackson would stop haunting him and reminding him of his biggest mistake. If he hadn't killed Jackson, if he only killed Clara instead and took her out of the picture, would they be happy together now?

Chapter 4: Delia

Delia, Becca, and Joel sat around the rectangular, oak kitchen table, which was covered in dishes: plates full of scrambled eggs, fried potatoes, fresh fruit, and bagels, a steaming metal carafe filled with fresh coffee, and a tea kettle. Delia reached for the tea kettle and grabbed a bagel. As she spread cream cheese on the bagel, Joel cleared his throat. Delia looked up expectantly, waiting for Becca or Joel to speak first. She noticed Becca avoided making eye contact with her.

"Delia, you know Becca and I didn't mind having you stay with us while you tried to get back on your feet," Joel said, pausing to take a sip of his coffee, although the steam rising from it made it apparent the coffee was still quite hot.

"We know you've had a rough few months, losing your mom, and…" Joel trailed off, perhaps unsure how much he should rehash about the events that transpired. "Anyways, we care about you and have tried to help you as much as we can, but we think it's time you try to piece your life together. We understand you need to find a job and need more time to be able to afford a place of your own, but we would like to set a deadline for when you should move out…"

Joel continued speaking, but Delia barely listened. She knew it was coming, but still felt uncomfortable with how it had been brought up. Joel sounded so formal as he asked that she move out soon. She glanced at Becca, who smiled awkwardly at her and quickly looked away. It bothered her that Becca hadn't been the one to come forward and tell Delia that they wanted her to move out. Of course, Delia was friends with both of them, but if she hadn't been best friends with Becca first, she probably wouldn't have become close to Joel. It hurt that Becca avoided the difficult topic. Delia suspected that Becca asked Joel to break the news to her.

Delia realized Becca and Joel were both looking at her now, as if they were waiting for her to say something. *Shit. What was the last thing Joel said? Something about a deadline for me to move out?*

Delia may have been uncomfortable and slightly hurt by the situation, but as a former police officer, she knew how to hide her emotions in stressful circumstances.

"Right. You both know I've been looking for a new job for a while now. I haven't found anything I would enjoy. I don't want to return to being a police officer. I'm not even sure they would take me back," Delia said.

Becca smiled sympathetically. "I'm sure Will would re-hire you as a security guard working at that apartment complex."

Delia sighed loudly. "Yes, he would want to help me. But I don't think I can go back to that. The only tolerable part of the job was that he was a great boss and it resulted in our friendship. Besides that, I couldn't stand the job."

Becca opened her mouth to say something else, probably what she thought would be another helpful suggestion, but Delia put up her hand to stop her before she could speak.

"Don't worry, Becca. I'll figure it out."

"Well, I was only going to say—what if you started your own private investigator business?" Becca suggested, biting her lip.

Delia wasn't used to seeing Becca so unsure of herself. Usually, Becca was the epitome of confidence and self-assurance. Delia supposed she hadn't made things easy on her and Joel lately, so she couldn't blame Becca for being hesitant to voice her opinion.

Delia pursed her lips. "Starting my own investigative business? I don't know about that, but I appreciate the idea."

Becca shrugged. "It was just an idea. I know you'll find whatever you're looking for eventually."

Delia nodded and stood from the kitchen table, leaving her bagel untouched.

Becca and Joel both stared at her quizzically.

"You aren't going to eat?" Joel asked, a hint of annoyance in his voice. He cooked the food for the brunch and was more than likely annoyed with her for not eating.

"Sorry," Delia said, grabbing her bagel smeared with cream cheese and wrapping it in a napkin. "I'll eat in my room. Thanks for the food." She paused. "And don't worry, I promise I'll move out soon."

Delia shuffled back to the guest bedroom, shut the door, and sat down at her desk. She took a small bite of her bagel. She was starving

20 minutes ago, but now felt too agitated to eat. Not agitated with Becca and Joel—she understood why they wanted her to move out and that she was close to overstaying her welcome. No, she was annoyed with herself for falling into such a slump. It was unlike her. She thought back to the days when she was a police officer and threw herself into every case she worked on. Even when she worked as a security guard, she worked long hours and put everything she could into her job. But now, what was she doing? Sitting in her best friend's spare bedroom eating a bagel with her dog? Even worse, she had no savings to speak of and no potential job opportunities.

Delia nibbled her bagel and Lily jumped up from her dog bed when she realized Delia had food. Lily whined by Delia's feet, hoping Delia would give in and throw the entire bagel to her.

She knew Becca was right. Delia opened her laptop and powered it on. She clicked on her favorite web browser and paused, typing *private investigator companies*. A few sites with job postings like indeed and glassdoor popped up, but that wasn't what she was searching for. She continued scrolling until she found an article that looked promising: *How to Start Your Own Private Investigator Company*.

She browsed the article and continued searching the Internet for similar articles. She grabbed one of her notebooks from the desk and made a list. Before she did anything else though, she needed to hire a partner. It would be preferable if she could find an experienced private investigator who could teach her the ropes. Although Delia had nearly a decade of experience working as an NYC police officer, she still wasn't sure she possessed the skills and knowledge to become a successful PI.

As Delia continued looking into the requirements to become a licensed PI, she learned that New York was one of the most difficult states to obtain a PI license. However, she wouldn't let this fact deter her. She would buckle down and throw herself into this next endeavor. She already had a Bachelor's Degree in criminal justice, which could only help her chances. Maybe she should take a few more criminal justice classes to refresh her knowledge. After all, she graduated from college more than 10 years ago.

She conducted several hours' worth of research about starting a small business and decided on the name *Wilson Investigative Services*. She filled out the Articles of Organization, submitted the paperwork, and paid the $200 fee to the New York Department of State. She also had to hire a registered agent and obtain an Employer Identification Number or EIN.

Delia sat back in the chair, staring at her notebook, feeling slightly overwhelmed and nervous, but excited for the first time in months. She could do this. And if she succeeded, if she worked cases involving missing persons or domestic abuse, she could prevent horrific things from happening. Delia wanted what she had always wanted, ever since she decided she wanted to become a police officer. She wanted to help people. To stop evil from wreaking havoc. To ensure the greater good always won. She knew it was an impossible feat, since she failed in so many regards, but it wouldn't stop her from moving forward. *Maybe I can atone for my mistakes. So, Jackson, Clara, Jerry... all the people I let down... didn't die in vain.*

Chapter 5: Edgar

Edgar sat alone in the darkness. He wasn't sure when he had last eaten and didn't know how much time had passed since he was sent to solitary confinement. He felt his way through the black room to the door and banged his fists on the door. His throat was hoarse from screaming. He wasn't sure if the room was soundproof, but no one came when he screamed.

After the second or third day, he felt a presence near him in the tiny cell. He heard the sound of footsteps coming toward him and quelled the urge to scream yet again. Who was in the cell with him?

Edgar cried out, "Who's there? How did you get in here?"

He heard a soft chuckle as a hand landed on his shoulder and made him yelp. A familiar stench suddenly overpowered the room.

"Edgar, who else would be in here with you? The only way in is through the door," Jackson said.

Edgar sighed in relief. "Oh, it's you."

Jackson snorted. "Yes, here to keep you company so you don't go insane. Although, I'm not sure what it means that you're seeing me more and more. Maybe you're already insane."

***

Edgar's week in solitary confinement ended at last. When the guard came to bring him back to his cell, Edgar dragged his feet, keeping his head down as he walked. Being alone in a prison cell was bad enough, but being stuck in solitary confinement was much worse. Edgar wondered if there was a limit on how long he was legally allowed to be in solitary confinement because he became unhinged after seven days. He hadn't been able to leave the cell, which meant no exercise, no time outside, no human interaction, or any form of entertainment that he was normally allowed, for seven days. Edgar's sanity spiraled downward due to the sensory deprivation. It was hell, a torture unlike any he had yet endured.

Having Jackson with him hadn't helped at all either. In fact, the confusion Edgar experienced upon seeing Jackson made things worse.

When he returned to his cell, his eyes pricked with tears as he saw the few possessions he was allowed in prison and the space that had been his home for several months. It also appeared brighter compared to the darkness he was immersed in for the past week. His eyes watered from the dim lights as he tried to adjust to seeing the tiniest amount of light again.

The guard placed a tray of food in his cell and Edgar immediately grabbed it. Although the meal looked depressing, Edgar was starving after only being allowed one meal per day for seven days. The tray held a fork, a slice of bread, baked beans, and two, plain overcooked hot dogs, but it looked like a feast to Edgar.

"Shit, you're like a wild animal," the guard said, chortling as he exited the cell. "You can eat in your cell today. You'll be allowed back in the chow hall tomorrow."

Edgar barely bobbed his head in acknowledgement, already shoveling the beans into his mouth with the fork. The guard stood outside the cell, staring at Edgar in disgust as he quickly demolished the meal. After Edgar finished eating, he sat on his bed, relishing the relative comfort compared to the bed in solitary confinement.

He pulled out a book, excited about the prospect of partaking in luxuries like reading after seven days of being deprived of such things. He quickly became lost in the world he read about, enjoying the perfect form of mental escapism while he was physically trapped. At least his mind could wander to other places. He could still dream of far-off countries, even if he could never visit them. The thought made him nauseous. He rushed over to the toilet. As soon as he knelt down on the cool floor, he expelled his lunch. Chunks of hot dog and beans floated in the toilet bowl and the sight made him vomit again.

Edgar wiped his mouth with the back of his hand and washed his hands in the sink. What was wrong with him? Maybe he ate too fast earlier. He had barely eaten in a week, so that would explain his nausea. It was probably too much for his stomach to handle.

He shakily walked over to his bed to recover.

The guard called out, "Hey! Are you okay in there?"

"Yes, just feeling a little sick," Edgar replied.

"Okay, let me know if you need to see a doctor," the guard said and went back to patrolling the hallway.

He laid down and closed his eyes, deciding rest was necessary. He barely slept while in solitary confinement. Nightmares consumed him each night, so he avoided sleeping and knew he was headed down a dangerous path if he didn't sleep soon. Besides, if he was unconscious, he didn't have to think about the fact that he was stuck in prison with no way out and this was how every day would unfold for the rest of his life. He would never see the outside world again, besides the enclosed courtyard at the prison, and that didn't count as freedom.

He drifted off to sleep and slept without dreaming for the first time in a while. What felt like minutes later, he was roughly shaken awake by a different guard than the one who led him back to his cell earlier in the day. Edgar wondered how long he slept. Long enough for a shift change apparently. He wearily opened his eyes and blinked rapidly.

"Wake up, bud. You have a visitor here to see you."

Edgar stared at the guard, his eyebrows scrunching together in confusion. "A visitor? Is it Delia?"

The guard shook his head no.

No one had visited him since he had been in prison, other than the several times Delia stopped by to harass him when he was first arrested. He assumed she gave up and returned to New York. *If it wasn't Delia, then who was it? Who would want to visit me? My parents are dead, Jackson is dead, and Liam is gone too…*

The guard smiled. "Come on, I'll take you to the visitor's center."

He handcuffed Edgar's hands together and motioned for Edgar to follow him down the long hallway. Edgar was still half-asleep and for a moment wondered if he was dreaming. The guard brought him to a table where a man sat, presumably waiting for him. The man had curly dark hair that came to just past his chin, dark brown, almost black eyes, and tanned skin. He smiled brightly when he saw Edgar and waved.

Edgar stared at the mysterious man, wondering who he was. Was he supposed to know him? Someone from his past he forgot about, maybe? Or a fan from *Dispatching David*? Although Edgar regained most of his memories after his accident and largely recovered from his amnesia, he still wondered what memories were hidden in the depths of his subconscious, buried until they saw fit to emerge.

"Okay, you have an hour to visit. No physical contact. And no violence or the visit will be terminated," the guard said, looking directly at Edgar with a warning in his eyes.

Edgar sat down in the chair opposite his unexpected visitor and the guard stepped away to give them some privacy. The mystery man leaned forward eagerly.

"Edgar! I can't believe it's you. I'm so excited that we're finally able to see each other after all these years. Although, of course I wish it was under better circumstances," he said, chuckling.

Edgar frowned. "Sorry… who are you?"

The man smiled broadly. "David." He leaned forward slightly more and whispered, "I'm an old friend."

Edgar's frown deepened. "I don't recognize you. Where do we know each other from?"

"My apologies. I shouldn't have assumed you would remember me. It was a long time ago. We were friends when we were kids. We lived on the same street and used to play together. We grew apart and lost touch as we grew up, but I never forgot you."

Edgar raised an eyebrow. "Wow, I'm sorry I don't remember you. I don't remember much of my childhood. It was difficult, to say the least."

David nodded in understanding. "That's okay. When I saw your name on the news and found out what happened, I wanted to visit you. I knew I had to see you. After I heard about your parents—well, I thought you might want someone to be there for you."

"I didn't have a lot of friends as a kid. How did we know each other?"

David smiled warmly. "I lived down the block from you. Your mom used to take us to Lake Harriet for picnics."

Edgar vaguely remembered at least one picnic with his mom at the lake. But had there ever been another child with them? The memory was fuzzy at best.

"I appreciate you visiting me," Edgar said, choosing his words carefully. "Do you still live around here?"

"No, I moved away. That was why we lost touch. I live in North Carolina now. Near the mountains."

"And you traveled all the way to Minnesota to see me?"

"Yeah, it seemed like the right thing to do."

Edgar's eyes narrowed in consternation. He didn't trust David. He suspected there were many people who wanted to harm him after the publicity he received from the murders. *David*, or whoever he really was, was probably trying to obtain information from him. Or maybe he was one of those true crime freaks who wanted to get close to a notorious criminal. Whatever the reason for David's visit, Edgar wouldn't fall for it. He wasn't stupid. He had almost evaded capture after committing multiple murders, after all.

"Not to be rude, but quite a few crazy people have tried visiting me, writing me letters, and contacting me. I'm not sure I believe you. This came out of nowhere."

"I understand. But our childhood friendship isn't the only reason I came here," David said.

Edgar sighed heavily. *Here it comes. The real reason David visited him.* "Okay. What else?"

"I'm going to help you escape," David said, smirking slightly at the look on Edgar's face.

"What?!" Edgar exclaimed, wildly looking around the room to make sure no one heard him. "Don't say that in here! I was released from solitary confinement today and I have no intention of going back there."

David's smile grew. "Don't worry so much, Edgar. I'm going to help you. I'll be back next week to see you again." David stood from his seat. "I'm glad we were finally able to see each other again," he said, appraising Edgar. "You aren't what I expected. Or what I remembered. But that was a long time ago. Friends for life, right?"

Edgar shook his head. "I don't know what sort of crazy 'plan' you have in mind, but this is the most secure prison in Minnesota. It's not like anyone can easily break out. No one has ever escaped."

"You don't need to break out of the prison. Not exactly. You don't need to decide right this second, but think about it, okay? Do you want to spend the rest of your life in here, Edgar? I'm sure that's not what you want. That's not what *I* would want."

"I'll consider it," Edgar finally conceded.

The guard approached them. "Your time's up. Say goodbye to your friend, Edgar."

"Next week?" David asked with a wretched smile.

Edgar dipped his head in acknowledgement and the guard led him out of the visitor's room and back to his cell. It hadn't been an hour, but he wasn't going to complain. He worried that if he said anything or complained, then the guards or prison warden would take away his visiting privileges.

As Edgar was locked in his cell once again, he sat on his bed pondering the events that transpired. Was David really an old friend from his childhood? How could he find out if he told the truth and they knew each other when they were kids? And the most important question of all: should he trust David if it meant he could escape?

Chapter 6: Delia

Delia, I'm sorry, but you aren't one of the police officers on this case, as much as you wish you were involved. You can't be anymore," Officer Dan said.

Delia adjusted her cellphone in her hand and sighed loudly. "I know, but I want an update. Does Edgar have a trial date set? Who will be brought forward as a witness for the case? And what—"

"As a regular citizen, you don't have the authority to know that information," Officer Dan replied. "I understand this has been hard for you, especially because it was one of your old cases, but it's no longer under your jurisdiction. The chief won't hesitate to block any future calls or emails. Please don't contact us again, Delia."

The phone line went quiet and Delia realized Officer Dan ended the call. *Great. Now what am I supposed to do? What do normal people do when they're trying to find out more information about an ongoing police investigation involving a notorious serial killer?*

Delia was used to the advantages police officers had, being privy to information about cases. She would have to adjust her methods to find out the information she needed in more creative ways. Most people tended to ignore the horrific things that happened in the world and pretended serial killers didn't exist. But Delia knew better. She saw the worst of humanity. She had looked into Edgar's eyes and knew something was off— suspected that he was a killer —but hadn't been able to prove it in time. No matter how much she tried to move on or forget about the case, it would haunt her forever and remain her biggest regret. It was why she had become obsessed with Edgar. Finding out everything she could about him, meticulously reading any online articles that mentioned his name, and continuously going over the details of the Birkman case. She couldn't let it go.

Delia went to the bank when it opened at 8:00 a.m. to take out a small business loan. She had registered her business already, but she needed a business bank account and a loan to cover her expenses. She hoped that soon she would be getting cases and be able to pay back the loan. After several other phone calls and errands related to her new business, she sat in her bedroom, contemplating what to do next. She glanced at her checklist and groaned. She needed a break.

Delia placed her phone on the nightstand and stood from where she sat cross-legged on her bed. Lily jumped up, tail wagging rapidly.

"Okay, let's go on a walk, Lil," Delia said, grabbing the leash from the closet and pulling Lily out of the room.

Delia walked Lily around the neighborhood for 20 minutes, hoping the fresh air, exercise, and quality time with her dog would help clear her mind. She had searched for a partner for her private investigator business, but hadn't found someone yet. She wondered if she would find someone competent and trustworthy. It was obvious from the several interviews she conducted already that no one would live up to Jerry, but she also knew no one could replace him for a different reason. Besides the fact that they worked together, they became friends after getting to know Jackson and subsequently trying to solve his murder. Nothing beat a partner who was also your friend.

Delia circled back around the neighborhood and checked the time on her phone. It was 9:35 a.m. Joel was at work for the day, but Becca had been at home writing in her home office when Delia left for her walk. If she headed back to the house now, maybe she could convince Becca to take a break from writing so they could chat and eat breakfast together.

When Delia approached Becca and Joel's 50-year-old red brick house, she did a double take at the open garage door. *Didn't I shut the garage when I left?* she wondered. She always closed it as a security precaution because Becca and Joel left the door in the garage that led into the house unlocked at all times, so if the garage door was open, anyone could walk into the house. Delia paused in the garage. As far as she could tell, nothing looked out of place.

Delia unclipped the leash from Lily's collar and picked her up. She tentatively opened the door and carried Lily inside the house, cradling her in her arms as she cautiously swept the perimeter. She didn't usually carry her gun with her, especially if she was doing a regular activity like taking her dog on a walk, so her gun was tucked away in the drawer of her nightstand. But maybe she was being paranoid. She tried to reason with herself. *Just because I left the garage door open, that doesn't mean anyone is inside the house. Becca is fine. I'm being cautious.*

"Becca?" Delia called out, carefully stepping into the hallway and walking toward the cozy sitting area. She glanced at the large, gray stone fireplace and black couch, noting everything looked normal so far. At this point, Lily squirmed in her arms, forcing her to let go. She hated being carried for more than a few minutes. Lily sprinted toward Becca's office, presumably to greet Becca. Delia followed her and stumbled into the office, instantly seeing that Becca wasn't there. The computer was on and the Word document Becca had been typing in was still open. *Okay, that's kind of weird. Unless she went to the bathroom? Or to the kitchen to grab a snack?*

Delia looked across the hall to the only bathroom in the house. The door was open. "Becca?" she called again, louder this time. "Where are you?"

The bathroom door was slightly ajar, so she shoved it open all the way, but no one was in there either. Delia frantically ran to the end of the hall where the master bedroom was located. "Becca!" she yelled as Lily ran after her. The master bedroom was empty also.

Fuck. Where is she?

The only two remaining rooms were the guest room Delia occupied and the kitchen. It seemed unlikely that Becca would be snooping around in the guest room since it was Delia's temporary room, but she checked the room to be thorough in her search. She opened the nightstand drawer and grabbed her gun, pulling out the ammunition and making sure the gun was loaded. She turned off the safety and stalked toward the last room to check for Becca. As she slowly entered the kitchen and surveyed the space, she realized Becca wasn't home.

She tried to suppress the panic intensifying in her chest. Becca could have left the house for a multitude of reasons. Maybe she decided to go on a walk. Or she could have plans with a friend or with Joel that she forgot to mention. Even though she wasn't home and hadn't notified Delia, that didn't mean something happened to her. She sprinted back into Becca's office, deciding she would go back through each room and inspect everything more carefully this time. If she didn't find anything suspicious, then she would call Becca and check in to make sure she was okay. Then, she could call Joel and ask if he knew where Becca went.

Delia inspected Becca's office first. The first time she went through each room so quickly, in a panic, that she hadn't noticed there was a note on Becca's desk with something else placed next to it. At a glance, the note looked as if it could belong to Becca—maybe notes for whatever book she was currently working on—but when Delia read the note, an icy chill crept down her spine.

The note was handwritten, but it was obviously not from Becca.

Delia,

I'm sure you've noticed your friend Becca is missing. I've always been a fan of playing games and this one is sure to be fun. For me, at least. Maybe not for you and Becca. I've left five clues for you to find her. The only catch is, if you don't agree to my rules, you will lose the game. Don't go to the police and don't do anything stupid. I've taken her somewhere secure for now, but unless you do as I say, you won't ever see Becca again.

Ezra Bliftin

Delia's heart beat so fast she thought it was going to burst out of her chest. *No. Not Becca.* This was all her fault. Her head spun as she tried to fight her worry and anxiety about Becca's wellbeing and think clearly. What if the person who wrote the note was bluffing or playing a sick joke on her? There was a possibility Becca wasn't going to be harmed. She couldn't take the chance though. Delia knew how many psychopaths there were in the world and would never forgive herself if Becca was killed. Neither would Joel...

She tried to clear her head and evaluate the note. She had no clue who Ezra Bliftin was. She would search the name later. As Delia scanned the note again, she noticed the object sitting next to the note, which hadn't registered to her. It was a doll with short blue hair and buttons sewn on for the eyes. It reminded her of the doll from *Coraline*. The type of creepy doll you would see in a horror movie that would probably come to life at night and murder you and your entire family. She avoided touching it, knowing it would be evidence. She wondered what the significance of the doll was. Becca had blue hair at one point. Maybe it was supposed to be her?

She whipped out her phone and called Becca. First, she needed to confirm if she could reach her friend. The phone rang and then went to voicemail. Delia left a voicemail asking Becca to call her back and let her know she's okay.

Delia decided the next step was to call Joel and tell him what was going on. She wondered for a brief moment if she should wait a bit and verify Becca was missing, but decided Joel would want to know immediately if his wife was missing. Waiting wouldn't change anything. In fact, it may make what was already a dire situation worse.

The phone rang and her heart stuttered as Joel answered.

"Hello? Delia?"

"Hi Joel. I'm so sorry to call you during the middle of the workday, but—"

"What's wrong?" Joel asked, cutting her off, his voice frantic.

"How do you know something's wrong?" Delia said, laughing nervously.

"You wouldn't call me at work unless there was an emergency." Joel paused. "Right?"

"Um, well…"

"Delia, you're scaring me. What's wrong? Is Becca okay? I haven't been able to get ahold of her all morning," Joel responded, the panic in his voice becoming more evident with each word.

Delia inhaled deeply and let the air out in a loud *whoosh*. "I took Lily on a walk this morning like usual, but when I returned to your house, the garage door was open. I checked every room, but Becca isn't home. I don't think she left the house willingly."

"What?" Joel practically screamed. "Why did you say that? Did something else happen?"

"There's a… a note. I found it on the desk in her office. I think someone kidnapped her."

"Oh my God, why didn't you lead with that, Delia? For God's sake. I'm coming home," Joel said, abruptly ending the call.

Delia stared at her phone for a minute, trying to calm down. She needed to be cool and collected for Joel. He would be a mess. Becca and Joel were high school sweethearts. They had been together since they were 17 and spent nearly two decades together. Delia watched them go through everything together and couldn't bear to think of how much pain Joel would be in if anything happened to Becca, not to mention how she would cope.

After what seemed like only a few minutes to Delia, Joel burst in through the garage door, demanding to see the note. He took it from Delia and quickly read it once, twice, again, scouring it for any clues about where Becca could possibly be.

"We need to call the police. You haven't called them yet, have you?" Joel asked.

"No, I haven't. I called you first because I wanted to make sure Becca hadn't gone somewhere. But the note says not to contact the police. I don't know if it's smart, Joel. We don't know who took her or why," Delia said emphatically.

Joel laughed harshly. "I know you're saying that because you don't trust the police as much after what happened with Edgar. It's our best option right now. We *need* to find Becca and make sure she's okay. Who would do this? Who would want to hurt her? Do you have any idea who Ezra Bliftin is?"

Delia shook her head. "I was hoping you would know. We will figure it out."

Joel inspected the doll on the desk and cringed. "What's up with this doll?"

Delia shook her head, not stopping Joel as he grabbed his phone and dialed 911 to file a missing person's report. Delia heard him mention the note and the doll and the fact that the garage door was open. Nothing else appeared to be out of place or missing. Joel hung up with the police officer and looked at Delia.

"They need to come here to inspect the crime scene, secure the evidence, and question us. You need to stay here with me and tell them what happened, since you're the one who found the note and the doll," Joel explained.

"Okay," Delia said slowly. She placed her hand on Joel's shoulder and smiled sympathetically. "I promise Becca will be okay. We *will* find her."

Joel nodded, gulping loudly in an attempt to stop his tears. "Okay."

"Hold on a minute, let me put Lily in my room so she won't be in the way of the investigation."

When she returned to the living room, she joined Joel on the couch. He was staring at his phone. As Delia tried to figure out what to say to comfort him, the doorbell rang.

"Are you ready for this?" she asked gently.

"Yes," he replied, putting his phone in his pocket.

Delia noticed what Joel had been staring at before he put his phone away. The lock screen background was a photo of Becca at the lake from one of their many outings there last summer. She smiled brightly, carefree and beautiful, in an ankle-length flowing white dress that only she could pull off. Her hair was dyed magenta and fell to her shoulders, one of the longer lengths she tried. Delia's eyes pricked with the warning that she was about to cry, but she swallowed her fear and anxiety and willed herself to stay strong.

Delia may have lost almost every person she loved, but she would not lose Becca. She was determined to find her and bring her home safely. Besides, she thought about it the entire time since she found the note from the kidnapper. Although she hadn't said anything to Joel yet, Delia knew who kidnapped Becca. He clearly used a fake name, but there was only one person that made sense. Who would come after

Delia and kidnap her best friend? Who would be sick and twisted enough to break into Becca and Joel's house and leave a note and a creepy doll and demand the police not be involved? It was Edgar.

Chapter 7: Edgar

As the days passed, Edgar fell into a routine and wondered if David would follow through on his promise to visit again. Did he have a plan? Or was he trying to get his hopes up only to have them crushed again?

Edgar dove into reading any interesting book he could find in the well-stocked prison library, worked out in the prison gym, did push-ups in his cell, ran around the prison courtyard during his brief time outside each day, and filled his days with every activity he was allowed to participate in, so he could attempt to strengthen his body and mind. He pondered his options. Regardless of whether David was who he claimed, Edgar wanted to escape prison. He supposed he needed to trust this strange man if he wanted any chance of leaving.

Edgar didn't think he would survive a life sentence in prison. He spent most of his time alone. His only social interaction was the bare minimum from the prison's guards. Once in a while, if he was being escorted to the chow hall or to the outdoor courtyard, another prison inmate would yell something obscene at him. He supposed being accused of multiple murders made him a target, so he understood why no one wanted to eat with him or play card games with him. Still, it would have been nice to have a friend. Or someone to talk to. He never thought he would miss having a genuine human connection with someone because he usually thought of himself as a tough, independent man. A loner. But now he knew that wasn't true. And honestly, he would kill for a friend right now.

Edgar spent too many hours thinking about all the ways he could be killed. He was constantly fearful of the other inmates and anxious every time someone stepped too close to him. One reason he worked out so often was to build up his strength and endurance in case someone attacked him. He wanted to be able to fight back. Since he didn't have any of his preferred weapons in prison, he needed to learn how to use his body as a weapon. It was his best option for survival. He didn't want to die in this hellhole and never see the outside world again. That was what he feared the most.

If a fellow prison inmate shanked him in the shower, stabbed him in the throat with a fork in the chow hall, or choked him to death because he wasn't strong enough to fight them off, his life would be as much of a waste as the rest of the people locked in here. Edgar was better than them. He wasn't a petty criminal; he was a criminal mastermind. It wasn't his fault he ended up in this place. His thoughts circled back to Delia for the hundredth time since he was arrested. It was probably unhealthy for him to constantly ruminate over what happened, since nothing could be done about it now, but he found himself contemplating the many delicious ways he could kill her and exact his revenge. He needed to escape, if only so he could kill Delia.

Chapter 8

I glanced in the backseat of my shitty 2001 white sedan to make sure Becca was still unconscious. I had entered the house after Delia carelessly left the garage door opened. I didn't even need to break in. The door in the garage that led into the house was unlocked. After that, it had been a simple matter of finding which room of the house Becca was in and knocking her unconscious. She was small and weak. No match for me. It surprised me how easy the whole thing had been. And now I was sure I would get away with it.

It was only a six-hour drive from NYC to Portland, but I was anxious the entire drive. I kept checking the rearview mirror and side mirrors to see if anyone was following me. I waited for the sound of a police car's siren to come blasting from behind me. But it didn't happen.

Traffic could be terrible in NYC and Becca didn't live in the city. I drove further out to find her. She and her husband lived in the suburbs, where houses were more affordable and there were supposedly less crimes. I chuckled as I thought about it. I wasn't sure what the exact statistic was for home break-ins and kidnappings, but I had just added one more to the total.

Chapter 9: Delia

Delia and Joel sat in silence, waiting in the police station closest to Becca and Joel's house. Delia was thankful that it wasn't her old precinct, as she wasn't in the mood to deal with her former co-workers or the police chief. They had waited for twenty minutes already. Delia knew how these types of things went and tried her best to reassure Joel this was a normal part of the process. She hoped it comforted him to have her there because she understood how to file a missing person's report. Time was of the essence when dealing with a missing person. In most missing person's cases, the police department would ask to wait 24-72 hours before filing an official report. But the note, creepy doll, and concerning circumstances surrounding Becca's disappearance changed things. This was an extreme case and the report needed to be filed as soon as possible.

They had already spoken to police officers at the house, explained what happened, shown them the crime scene, and given them the evidence. Afterwards, the police officers had asked them to come into the station to file the police report.

When an overweight, balding, police officer with kind green eyes finally approached them, Joel looked like he was on the verge of a breakdown.

"Hello, I'm Karl," the police officer said, extending his hand and shaking first Joel's hand, then Delia's. "If you'll follow me, please, hopefully we can sort out this situation."

Delia and Joel followed Karl to the other side of the police station, where the "offices" were partitioned with flimsy, folding walls, offering only a small semblance of privacy. One of the offices in the middle was where Karl stopped and gestured for the two of them to sit in the plastic chairs across from his desk. His desk was littered with soda cans, energy drinks, and fast-food wrappers, not exactly painting a picture of organization and togetherness to Delia and Joel.

Karl grabbed a form from his desk. Delia thought it was a miracle he could find anything in the mess, but kept quiet, surveying the area with muted disgust. Her face softened when she noticed the only framed picture on Karl's desk, which appeared to be an old wedding picture of a slimmer, younger Karl with more hair, hand in hand with a curvy, brunette woman whose hair was styled in curls piled on top of her head.

Delia pointed to the picture. "Is that your wife?" she asked, smiling, hoping to start off on the right foot with Karl, so he would be eager to help them.

Karl returned the smile. "Yup, that's my Marissa. Still as beautiful as she was 20 years ago," he replied fondly.

Joel attempted to smile, but tears spilled from his eyes. Delia placed her hand on his shoulder comfortingly and turned back to Karl.

"Is it okay if we start filing the missing person's report?" she asked.

Karl nodded. "Of course. To start, I'll need the missing person's full name, date of birth, and home address."

Joel answered Karl's questions as best he could with Delia chiming in whenever necessary to help, not only because Joel was barely keeping it together, but also because Delia had been the one to discover the note and doll. After Joel and Delia described Becca's physical appearance and the outfit she wore this morning, Joel passed along a recent photo of Becca. Delia suggested he bring it, so the photo could be added to the report.

"I'm sorry you're going through this," Karl told Joel, brushing aside a few soda cans on his desk. "But we will do everything we can to ensure Becca returns home safely. You reported the case quickly. The details you provided, along with the photograph, and the items from the crime scene, will all help us with the case."

Delia wondered why he didn't brush the soda cans into the small, wire trash basket next to his desk.

"Thank you," Joel managed to say quietly, his face a tear-streaked mess, his eyes blotchy and red.

"Now we need to question each of you separately—"

"Are you serious?" Joel said, outraged. "Are we suspects?"

Karl shrugged one shoulder. "It's typical protocol. Although Delia was the one who found the note and the doll, we need to rule her out as a suspect. And Joel, we will need to confirm that you were really at work this morning. If you have coworkers or supervisors who can serve as a witness that you were in the office today, then you will need to give us their contact information."

Delia and Joel both nodded.

"Delia, I'll question you first. Joel, you can wait here."

Delia followed Karl into a room at the back of the police station. Karl shut the door and motioned for her to take the seat across from him. Delia thought about how ironic it was that she was now on the other end of an interrogation after her years of working as a police officer. She sat in the metal folding chair and steeled herself for the conversation. She hadn't done anything wrong. She would be fine.

"Will you please take me again through what happened this morning?" Karl prompted, pulling out a tablet to take notes.

Delia explained for what felt like the dozenth time that she had left the house to walk her dog and returned to an empty house.

"Did you see anyone on your walk? Can anyone corroborate that you weren't home when Becca went missing?"

"I passed a few of the neighbors while I was walking around the neighborhood, but no one that I know personally. Can you check footage from the DAS cameras, if there are any in the neighborhood?" Delia knew that New York City used the Domain Awareness System (DAS) for surveillance across the city. There was a chance she had been recorded on her walk.

"Yup, we will look into it," Karl replied, making another note on his tablet. "What time did you return to Becca and Joel's house?"

"Around 9:35 a.m. I remember checking my phone as I walked up the driveway."

"You said the garage door was open and the house was unlocked?"

"Yes, I must not have shut the garage door when I left, and Becca and Joel always keep the garage door unlocked."

Karl remained silent as he typed on his tablet for a moment. "Did anyone else have a key to the house or a garage door opener?"

Delia paused. "I don't think so, but you'll have to ask Joel to be sure."

"So, you entered the house and searched for Becca. Then what?"

"I found the note and doll that the kidnapper left. I didn't touch anything because I knew it would contaminate the evidence. Then, I called Joel to tell him what was going on. He left work and called the police when he returned home."

"Why didn't you call the police first?" Karl asked, looking up from his tablet to make direct eye contact.

"I wanted to tell Joel Becca was missing before I did anything else. I didn't want to call the police without him."

"You don't have any idea who Ezra Bliftin is?"

Delia shook her head no and bit her bottom lip.

Karl made a few more notes and switched his tablet to sleep mode. "That's all for now. We don't have enough evidence to name a suspect yet, but we will be in touch if any more questions come up." He pulled out a business card and set it on the table. "Here's my contact information if you think of anything else that could be helpful."

"Actually, there is something else…" Delia said, hesitant if she should tell Karl what she was thinking. But why wouldn't she? If it would save Becca, then she had to do everything she could.

"I think—I *know* who did it," Delia said, choosing her words carefully. "It was Edgar Peterson," she paused, letting the information sink in, wondering if Karl recognized the name. Maybe he didn't. "The serial killer."

Karl's eyes widened in surprise. "The one who's waiting to go on trial for the murders of Jackson Birkman and his fiancée?"

"Along with several other murders, yes," Delia said.

Karl smiled patronizingly. "It couldn't have been him. I read an article about him this morning. He's in the Harriet Heights Maximum Security Prison, the most secure prison in Minnesota. I think you're mistaken, Delia."

Delia slammed her hand down on the wooden table, causing it to shake unsteadily. "Sorry," she muttered. "But I'm not mistaken. I'm the one who found Edgar when he was in hiding and I'm sure he blames me for his arrest. He kidnapped Becca in an attempt to get revenge."

"How could he have done that? Like I said, he's in a maximum-security prison. No one has ever escaped."

"He must have found a way! He's—he's very clever. Or maybe he has someone on the outside doing his dirty work for him. Maybe that's who Ezra Bliftin is. I'm not sure of the specifics yet, but it was him. Becca doesn't have any enemies. She's a kind, lovable person. She's a writer, for God's sake. Who would go after a writer?" Delia said furiously.

"I can see how it would make things simple if it was Edgar who kidnapped Becca. Or if he was somehow involved with her going missing. But we have no reason to believe it was him. I'll keep it in mind as we move forward with filing the report and commencing the search, but I think we should focus our energy on every possibility.

It's too early to name persons of interest or assume who's at fault if Becca *was* taken," Karl said.

Delia turned to leave. "I'll visit Edgar and prove it was him."

"I don't know if that's a good idea," Karl responded to Delia, scratching his chubby chin. "He's a very dangerous criminal."

Delia stood to leave. "Is that it then?"

Karl eyed her warily. "Yes, I need to question Joel now."

Karl let Delia exit the room in front of him since she was clearly in a hurry to leave. They walked back to Karl's office where Joel was waiting, anxiously tapping his foot. He stopped when he saw them.

"Please follow me, Joel, so I can ask you a few questions," Karl said.

"Okay."

Karl and Joel walked away to the interrogation room.

Delia sat in the unoccupied chair and pulled out her phone, staring at the picture she had taken of the note. She waited for Joel to return as she contemplated the clues. It had to be Edgar.

Karl and Joel entered the office 15 minutes later.

"Be sure to follow up with us in a few days if you haven't heard anything. We'll keep you updated with any leads. In the meantime, you can reach out to any of Becca's friends or family members who may know where she is. You can also post on social media with a photo of Becca and the details surrounding her disappearance and start a hotline number for people to call with tips," Karl said.

Delia exhaled loudly. "You don't need any further information?"

Karl shook his head. "That's it for now. If she's still missing in a few days, we will request her bank records, cell phone records, and social media account log-in information."

"Okay, thanks, Karl. We'll be sure to follow up soon if we don't hear from you," Delia responded.

Delia and Joel exited the police station and headed toward Delia's car.

***

The next day, Delia and Joel drove around the city hanging up missing person's posters with Becca's face on them. Delia also started a hotline, so if anyone had any tips about Becca and where she was, they could call in. The next thing she did was start a Facebook group asking anyone with information about Becca to come forward. She wasn't sure if hanging posters around the city would be helpful and knew that social media was becoming more relevant in cases now. Maybe they would be lucky and someone could help them.

When they returned to the house, Delia pulled out her phone and searched the name Ezra Bliftin. Zero results. As she continued searching different combinations of the name, Delia's phone dinged with a text notification. She eyed her phone warily and saw that the message was from a phone number she didn't recognize:

Delia, I know what you did. I warned you not to go to the police. Did you think I wouldn't find out? Or did you think I was bluffing about hurting Becca if you told anyone? Consider this a warning. Screw up again and I'll do much worse to her.

Delia trembled as she clicked on the image that was sent with the text. Becca was handcuffed to what appeared to be a metal pipe attached to a wall. The room was dimly lit and the image looked grainy. There was a knife glistening next to Becca's arm and a line of blood dripping down the blade. Delia gasped and tried to hide her phone so Joel wouldn't see, but she wasn't quick enough.

Joel grabbed the phone out of her hands, skimmed the text, looked at the image, and silently handed Delia's phone back to her. She expected him to be terrified or sad. Instead, his eyes gleamed with anger.

"I'm not going to let them hurt Becca," he said. "We have to find her."

After their conversation, Delia searched for the phone number online to see if anything came up for it. There were companies you could pay to determine whose name a phone number was registered to. Nothing came up when she searched for the phone number or when she tried adding "owner" and "user" after the phone number, so she paid a small fee to a highly-rated company who claimed they could trace the number. She knew the risks because if the phone number was quickly deactivated or transferred to another person, then the search might not be accurate. But she had to try.

The Long Shadow of Death

Chapter 10

Delia didn't listen to me when I warned her about going to the police. It wasn't my fault I had to punish Becca for Delia's insolence. I didn't hurt her severely, only enough to scare Delia and make her see that I was being serious. It's not like I wanted to do it. But I wanted Delia to understand that I'm not messing around. After I sent the image of Becca's arm where I cut her, I smirked picturing the look on Delia's face. I could only imagine how terrified she felt. It's only right after what she did, making me lose the love of my life.

Everything I'm doing now is for her—the woman I lost.

I want to make Delia pay. I want Delia to feel as hopeless as I did. If she doesn't do as I say, I swear to God I'm going to kill Becca.

Chapter 11: Edgar

You have a visitor," one of the guards said as they sidled up to Edgar's cell.

"David?" Edgar asked eagerly, perking up at the thought of his potential escape.

"Nope, not this time. Delia, I think her name was?" the guard said, shrugging his shoulders and unlocking the cell door with his key card.

Edgar's face seemed to redden and pale at the same time. She hadn't visited him since his arrest. Delia unsuccessfully tried to obtain a confession from him, but he would never confess, especially not to her. No matter what she did or how hard she tried, Edgar would never tell Delia the truth about the murders. He was surprised she would come back to see him after what he imagined had been several extremely disappointing visits. It had been a while, so he wondered what the sudden interest was in seeing him. *She couldn't have found any new evidence. Right?*

"You coming or what?" the guard snarled, stepping into the cell, handcuffs outstretched. "You don't have to see her if you don't want any visitors. It's one of your rights."

But curiosity had the better of him. He wanted to know what Delia wanted. Edgar nodded. "I want to see her," he said, holding out his hands for the cuffs.

The guard led him down the hallway to the visitor's room for the second time that month. "You know the rules," he said, stepping away to give them a bit of privacy.

Edgar sat to face Delia. Her normally curly red hair was sleek in a high ponytail, her green eyes focused and determined. She was wearing a gray blazer and matching pants.

"Hello, Delia," Edgar greeted her, smiling sinisterly.

Delia inclined her head toward him curtly.

"Well, are you going to tell me why you came all the way to Minneapolis? I'm assuming it's not because you missed me," Edgar said with a smirk.

Delia narrowed her eyes. Edgar was already getting to her, which made him smile more. It was too easy to toy with her. He welcomed the amusement to break up his monotonous days.

"My friend Becca is missing," Delia said simply, staring at him expectantly, as if she was waiting for a reaction.

Edgar's smile froze and he tilted his head to the side in confusion, wondering what that had to do with him. "And?"

"I know it was you," Delia said through gritted teeth, clenching her hands in her lap.

"How could it have been me, Delia? I've been here since April. I'm in a maximum-security prison with guards watching me 24/7, in case you haven't noticed," he said, gesturing at the guards standing in the room.

"I understand that, which is why I think you have someone on the outside you've been in contact with. Someone you're working with who kidnapped Becca."

"That's absurd," Edgar said, rolling his eyes. "Why would I go after your friend?"

"For revenge. For being involved in your arrest," Delia said, unclenching her hands and placing them on the table in front of her.

Edgar shook his head in amazement. "I can't believe you would think so lowly of me. Don't you know me at all by now, Delia?"

Now it was Delia's turn to roll her eyes. "Of course I do. This is *precisely* the type of stunt you would pull."

Delia pulled her cellphone out of her pocket and turned the screen toward Edgar so he could see the message she received from the blocked number. "I know whoever is working for you sent this. You better not fucking hurt her anymore."

Edgar stared at the photo Delia showed him. He rested his chin in his hands on the table and leaned toward Delia. "I'll admit I'm intrigued by this situation. But you're wrong this time. It wasn't me. I'm sure you've made plenty of other enemies though, so maybe you should contact the ones who aren't locked away in prison." His eyes glinted dangerously as he spoke.

"*I know it was you, Edgar,*" Delia said viciously, leaning forward, so their faces were only inches apart through the plexiglass wall separating them.

"Hey! Enough of that," one of the guards said, misinterpreting the reason why Edgar's and Delia's faces were suddenly both pressed up against the plexiglass. He shoved them apart and grabbed Edgar by his upper arm, forcing him to stand. "No kissing allowed," he said with a sarcastic laugh.

Edgar chuckled darkly at the irony of the situation. He couldn't remember the last time he kissed a woman. And he killed the only man he ever kissed.

Chapter 12: Delia

Delia sighed in exasperation, wondering if flying to Minneapolis to talk to Edgar in person had been worth it. In hindsight, maybe not. When she started her private investigator business, she had been forced to take out a small business loan from the bank. The cost of the flight and traveling had come from her loan. She could cover her business expenses for now, but the money wouldn't last forever.

Delia thought Edgar was involved in Becca's disappearance, but she had been stupid to assume he would admit to it. He was already in prison for multiple murders, so why would he confess to planning the kidnapping of her best friend?

She had already Google searched the name from the note left by Ezra Bliftin, Becca's assailant. But she searched again during the flight. To her disappointment, there were still zero search results. She assumed they were using a fake name, so she couldn't identify them. Otherwise, why was there no trace of them on Google? But why did they bother to leave a name at all? Was it a clue about their identity?

What was the significance of the name? She could contact one of her old co-workers from the NYPD 19th Precinct when she was back in NYC and ask them to search the name in the police database. Maybe they would be able to find something she couldn't.

She pulled up the screen on the window and looked outside. She always chose the window seat on planes if she could. She loved staring out the window and watching the world below soar by. The towns looked so tiny, lined with miniature homes and toy cars driving by. She knew flying gave some people anxiety, but Delia found it thrilling. She watched the cotton candy clouds float by as darkness descended. She had taken a late flight, which she had paid for with her credit card. She only stayed one night in Minneapolis. Delia thought back to her failed attempt to talk to the police chief at the Minneapolis Police Department in person while she was in Minnesota.

Delia entered the police station full of confidence, sure that they wouldn't turn her away if she showed up, as long as she didn't lose her cool and do something crazy. She couldn't blame them for not wanting her involved, but it still annoyed her that she wasn't privy to any new information regarding Edgar's potential conviction and upcoming trial. All she wanted was to make sure he was convicted and locked away forever, so the world was safe from him. She didn't want everything she had been through, everything she risked and lost to apprehend Edgar, to be for nothing.

When Delia walked into the police station, she was immediately stopped by a tall, athletic-looking black man.

"Hello, ma'am, can I help you with something?" he asked cordially.

At least he didn't know who she was.

"Yes, I would like to speak to the police chief."

"Regarding what? Civilians don't normally walk in here and ask to speak to him," the man said.

Delia smiled broadly, exuding friendliness and politeness. "I was one of the officers who assisted in the arrest of Edgar Peterson. I wanted to talk to the police chief regarding the investigation."

The man appraised her, most likely noting that she was dressed in civilian clothes and didn't appear to be a police officer. "Sorry, what did you say your name was?"

"It's Delia. Delia Wilson." She flashed her NY PI license at him for proof.

The man's eyes widened. Apparently he knew her name, even if he didn't know what she looked like.

"Oh, well, I apologize, but the police chief is actually out today, so he isn't available," he stuttered.

Delia brushed a few stray hairs from her face and looked the police officer in the eyes. "Look, I'm sure you know who I am and I don't know what the police chief told you about me, but this is urgent." Delia took a step closer and lowered her voice. "I think Edgar may have been involved in a kidnapping."

The man crossed his arms over his chest. "Okay, when did the kidnapping take place?"

"A few days ago," Delia said excitedly, hoping she could win him over.

"What? Edgar has been in prison for months…" the officer said, as his eyebrows scrunched together in confusion.

Delia huffed impatiently. "I know that, but I think he's working with someone on the outside. Someone who is continuing his work for him while he's locked away. This is why I need to talk to the police chief!"

"I'll pass along the message to him," the man said abruptly, turning his back on her and walking away.

"Wait!" Delia said, grabbing his shoulder to stop him.

He spun around, swiping her hand off his shoulder. "Ma'am, please don't touch me. Now I'm kindly requesting that you leave the station and don't return. Otherwise, I'll have to remove you from the premises forcefully and I think you know what will happen if you resist."

"Fine, but you're all making a terrible mistake," Delia said, turning on her heel and exiting the police station.

The plane was descending. The heavy woman next to her snored obnoxiously and Delia shuddered, thankful the flight was almost over.

After Delia grabbed her small duffel bag from the overhead compartment, she ordered an Uber. She hated driving to the airport, so she had left her car at home. She didn't want to ask Joel to pick her up from the airport because he was so overwrought. She didn't want to add to his stress. She still hadn't told him that she suspected Edgar was responsible for Becca's disappearance. She needed proof before she could tell him. Besides, no one else believed her, so why would Joel?

The Uber dropped her off at Becca and Joel's house. She entered the house to find Joel sitting on the couch wearing a pair of sweatpants and a plain gray T-shirt. She could have sworn it was the same outfit he wore when she left yesterday morning. He hadn't been to work since Becca had disappeared.

She greeted him with a small smile. "Hey, Joel. I'm back from my trip."

Joel looked up from the TV. It appeared he was watching a comedian's stand-up act. "Oh, it's been that long already?" He picked up his cellphone from the coffee table in front of him and glanced at the time. "Fuck, it really has." He stood from the couch, brushing popcorn crumbs from his sweatpants.

Delia stared at him, worried about his mental health. She may not be handling Becca's disappearance in the healthiest way possible, but she was holding herself together and maintaining the appearance of being alright. She knew they handled things differently. Delia was the type of person to spring into action, while Joel became emotional and could barely function while his wife was missing.

"When's the last time you ate?" Delia asked Joel, walking into the kitchen, opening the tiny pantry and then checking the fridge. "We need to buy groceries."

"I ate some popcorn," Joel mumbled, joining Delia in the kitchen to search for food.

Lily joined them, springing up from her perch on the couch when she realized Delia was home. Delia scratched Lily's head until she calmed down and grabbed a box of half-empty pasta from the pantry.

"Okay, well I'm cooking a late dinner. I don't think you've been eating enough and you need to take better care of yourself," Delia said firmly.

Joel scratched the stubble on his chin that was so unlike his usual clean-shaven look. "You're right. Thanks." He wandered back to the couch to resume his previous position and Lily followed him, perhaps sensing that he needed her comforting presence more than Delia did currently.

Delia cooked the pasta, found an unopened jar of pasta sauce and leftover sausage, then toasted and seasoned a few slices of bread for garlic bread. She never particularly enjoyed cooking, but it took her mind off of Becca, Edgar, and the multitude of other things she was obsessing over.

Delia made Joel leave the couch, so they could eat their late-night meal at the kitchen table together. They ate in silence. Joel cleared his plate, leaving Delia relieved that he still had an appetite. Delia washed the dishes, tidied up the kitchen and living room, and retreated to her bedroom with Lily following close at her heels.

As Delia sat at her desk creating a job posting and adding it to Craigslist, Lily sat in her dog bed, staring at her. She had already tried a few other job posting sites and was running out of places to look. Delia clicked "Post" on her listing and sat back, carefully re-reading it for the third time, satisfied.

My name is Delia Wilson. I'm a former NYC police officer and recently started my own private investigator business, Wilson Investigative Services. I'm currently searching for a partner to join me in this endeavor, preferably someone with a decade or more of experience. I need someone dependable, trustworthy, and diligent, with stellar communication, surveillance skills, research skills, and critical thinking. You should be trained to use a gun and have a concealed carry permit. You will be working closely with me and required to be knowledgeable about detective work for things like searching for missing persons, criminal activities, domestic violence cases, etc. Please respond directly to the job posting if you're interested and meet the criteria I listed. Thank you.

Delia hoped she would find a reliable partner soon, but decided to wait at least a week before making any decisions. That should give people plenty of time to find the job posting and apply, then she could sort through the applications and contact the top applicants, whoever seemed the most promising. She didn't want to become desperate and hire the first person who applied. Who knew what types of weirdos applied for jobs on Craigslist, after all?

Delia wearily stood from her chair and stretched her stiff body. For now, she needed to sleep. Maybe tomorrow things would be better.

***

When Delia woke, the sun already shone harshly through the sheer drapes in the room. She jumped out of bed, throwing on a clean pair of jeans and a T-shirt, and stumbled into the hallway, heading toward the kitchen. *Joel must be sleeping still*, she thought drowsily as she brewed a pot of water for tea. Once the stove was turned on, she stumbled half-asleep to the couch in the family room, turned on the TV, and watched the morning news while she ate a bowl of cereal. She checked her emails and was relieved to see one from the company she paid to trace the anonymous phone number.

The phone number was registered to Ezra Bliftin. Delia quickly read the rest of the email and set her phone back down on the table. She had already known that, but had hoped the phone would be registered to a different name, perhaps Ezra Bliftin's real name. It seemed he was being cautious and had taken measures to keep his true identity hidden from her.

As she pondered Ezra's true identity, she realized something was off. She froze; her hand still clutched her bowl as her heartrate sped up. *Where is Lily?*

She ran out of the family room, back into her bedroom, and checked Lily's dog bed, where she normally hung out during the day. She wasn't there. Lily wouldn't be with Joel. She always slept in Delia's room with her. She opened the bathroom door, knowing it was futile. Why would Lily have gone into the bathroom? She wasn't in the family room either. Delia even checked Becca's office, although the door had remained closed since she discovered Becca was missing, and Lily wasn't in there either.

She sank into the couch, her breathing coming faster and faster until she was sure she was having a panic attack. Sweat dripped down the back of her neck and she felt the anxiety crawling over her skin, like a spiderweb she couldn't quite brush off. She couldn't remember the last time she had a panic attack, but the familiar feeling certainly wasn't welcome. She leaned forward and put her head between her knees, willing herself to take slow, deep breaths until her heartbeat slowed down and she could think rationally.

Suddenly, something wet and rough brushed against her hand and she jolted upright. "Fuck!" she shouted, stumbling forward into Joel.

Lily jumped up onto her legs, thinking Delia was playing with her.

Joel looked flabbergasted. "Are you okay, Delia?" he asked, grabbing onto her shoulder to steady her so she didn't fall. He was strong and solid, otherwise she probably would have knocked him over.

"Yeah, I—I couldn't find Lily," Delia gulped loudly, as she smelled the scent of something burning coming from the kitchen. The water started boiling, but she hadn't added the tea bag or watched the time, so the water boiled away.

Joel reached down to pet Lily and let her lick his hand. "I heard her whining at your bedroom door this morning, so I took her outside. She had to use the bathroom. When we came back inside, she followed me into my bedroom, so when I went back to sleep, I decided to let her sleep with me. Sorry, I didn't think about—"

"No, it's fine. Really. I know she can be comforting. I overreacted. After Becca, I just—I assumed the worst."

Joel smiled in understanding and ran a hand through his disheveled hair. "Sorry again though. How about we go out for breakfast? Leaving the house for a bit will be good for both of us."

Delia paused to consider the suggestion. "That's a great idea," she agreed. "I need a few minutes to finish getting ready, then we can go."

Joel looked down at his sweatpants and laughed. "I guess I need to change clothes too."

30 minutes later, Delia and Joel were sitting at one of the tables in Delia and Becca's favorite café, which they frequently visited. The café had a wide assortment of breakfast and lunch foods, coffees, and teas from around the world. It was decorated in a nice, comforting style and had been owned by an elderly couple for many years.

As Delia munched on a croissant and sipped her tea, she finally felt herself calming down. "So, how's work doing without you? Was your boss understanding when you told them what was going on?" Delia asked, laughing awkwardly the second the words left her mouth. "Sorry, that was a dumb question. I didn't want to talk about—"

Joel shook his head, not minding the subject. "Yeah, he was fine with it when I explained I needed some time off. I have a lot of vacation time and personal time saved. Although I had hoped to use it for an anniversary trip with Becca in the fall."

Delia smiled gently. "Right. Thanks again for watching Lily while I was gone. I really appreciate it."

"No problem, I'll watch her any time. She's a weird little puggle, but she's great company."

Delia finished her tea and set the ceramic mug back on the table. "What are your plans for the rest of the day?"

Joel winced and Delia wondered if today was a date she should have remembered. She quickly scanned through all the memorable dates she could recall. Becca and Joel's anniversary was in October, so it wasn't that.

Joel finally spoke again. "I planned on surprising Becca with tickets to see *Wicked* on Broadway. The show is tonight."

"Wow, *Wicked*? That show's supposed to be great!" Delia said, momentarily forgetting the situation.

Joel stared at his coffee mug. "Yeah, it would have been a great date night. It's her favorite musical."

Delia reached across the table and squeezed Joel's hand. "You're such a thoughtful husband. Becca would have loved it."

Joel smiled sadly at Delia. "I wish I could have taken her to see it."

"You can take her to see it when we find her," Delia said. "Want to head home now? I was thinking we should blast some more posts on social media with photos of Becca and the details about the case. A lot of cases recently have been solved because of social media. I really think it could help."

"Great idea," Joel said, chugging his heavily sugared coffee that had become quite cold. "I'm glad I still have you, Delia. I don't know how I would be getting through this without you."

"Me too."

***

Several hours later, Delia and Joel had both made numerous posts in the Facebook group they had started related to Becca's disappearance. Delia also posted on Instagram, Twitter, and every other online platform she could think of. Joel checked in with the police station, but they didn't have any leads yet.

Delia looked at her cellphone and was surprised to see three new emails. She scanned through them, determining if any of them were important. The only one she cared about was the last email, which was sent by a man named Carter Chapman. His email was in response to her job posting. He was interested in a job interview.

"What's up?" Joel asked, noticing her distraction.

"Someone responded to the job posting I made. His name is Carter. He doesn't have the experience I was looking for in a partner though."

Joel frowned. "He doesn't meet your requirements? That's an automatic no."

"What if he's a good fit though? How will I know if I don't give him a chance?" Delia asked emphatically.

"A lot has changed the last few days. You need to be careful who you hire."

"I know; you're right." Delia brushed a stray curl from her face. "I'm not used to being in the public eye and after Becca's disappearance, I know I need to be especially cautious now."

"Do a background check on him before you hire him. And bring your gun with you to the interview in case he's a psycho."

Delia smirked. "I appreciate you being concerned about my safety, but I can handle myself. I've gotten out of some pretty crazy situations on my own."

"I know," Joel said quietly, shoving his hands into his pockets. "Maybe if she had taken self-defense classes or you trained her to use a gun, then Becca wouldn't be missing," he said.

"You can't think about it that way. But don't worry, as soon as we find Becca, I'm teaching her all my best self-defense moves and enrolling her in a gun certification class."

"Will you train me too?" Joel asked earnestly. "I want to be able to protect her if anything ever happens again."

"Sure." She would do whatever she could to protect both of them.

"Delia?"

"Yeah?"

"Do you think someone will call the hotline or comment in our Facebook group with information about Becca? You know more about this stuff than I do. What are the chances that they find her?" Joel asked hesitantly.

"I hope so. I need one good lead and then I'll go looking for her myself."

"Thanks, Delia."

Delia thought about Becca and wondered where she was, if she was scared and alone. She wondered how deep the cut to her arm had been and how long it would take before it became infected. How serious was her injury? And had they harmed her again since then?

Wherever Becca was and whoever had taken her, Delia hoped Becca was still alive. She couldn't bear to think about the alternative.

Chapter 13: Edgar

Edgar missed acting: the feeling of being on a stage or on a TV set surrounded by other actors and creative people, knowing everyone was counting on him, memorizing lines, the feeling of ecstasy when he nailed a role and truly understood the character he was portraying, the fame, the recognition—he missed it all. He longed for the life he used to have and all the things he hadn't appreciated back then. He did his best not to think about it, but it was hard to keep his thoughts away from dreaming about the future he always imagined for himself—the life of a Broadway star—night after night onstage in a theatre, ending shows to standing ovations. The dream had been within his grasp, barely out of reach, but it had been snatched away from him, along with all his other hopes for his future. But most of all, he longed for Jackson; his love he had destroyed.

Amidst all his daydreaming, Edgar questioned if David would come back to visit him or if it had all been a lie, some elaborate ploy to make him think he had a friend, or someone to help him. He had nothing better to do with his time than contemplate the meeting with David, then the visit from Delia. Edgar snickered as he thought about how Delia came all the way to Minneapolis to accuse him of kidnapping her friend. He had to admit; if he was capable of staging such a thing, it was a pretty great idea. It was a way to get to Delia. He wondered who *did* kidnap her friend. Perhaps another person she arrested or someone else whose downfall she helped orchestrate? He was sure Delia made plenty of enemies over the years in her profession, himself included. The thing was, if she let go of the case and forgot about it like the other police officers, detectives, and investigators, Edgar would have left her alone. But the way she kept coming at him, over and over, determined to bring about his demise, filled him with an anger he had only felt a few times in his life. The same anger that drove him to kill…

***

Edgar ate dinner at a table by himself in the chow hall, as he always did. A short man with a beard and neck tattoos stalked toward him.

"Hey," he said in a gruff voice.

Edgar stared at him, wary about the man's intentions. He didn't recognize him. He didn't have any friends or acquaintances in prison and he wasn't trying to make any. "Hello," he said cordially, not wanting to be rude, but wondering why the man approached him.

"My name's Tony. Max over there wants to talk to you," he said, pointing to the thin man with pale skin in the corner, who smiled menacingly.

Edgar shuddered, despite his best efforts to hide his fear. He had been in the maximum-security prison for long enough to know who not to cross. Although he tried to avoid everyone regardless of what they were in prison for or how normal they looked, he knew that Max was the toughest guy in there. Max was a serial killer convicted of killing nine people. Nine women who he stalked, raped, and then murdered. Max had formed his own gang in the prison and basically ran things. Many of the prison guards turned a blind eye to Max's illicit activities and the violent acts he committed. Edgar didn't have a clue why Max would want to talk to him. He was an angel compared to Max.

"Okay," he finally replied, deciding that agreeing to talk to him was probably the safest move. There were plenty of guards in the chow hall. Surely, one of them would intervene if Max tried to injure him. But he wondered if it was true. Would someone help him if Max tried to harm him?

Tony walked toward the corner of the chow hall and Edgar followed him. Max leaned nonchalantly against the wall, standing next to another man who was muscular, had a shaved head, and was in a protective, guarding stance. Tony jerked his head at Max.

"He'll talk to you," Tony said.

Max tilted his head in acknowledgement and turned to look at Edgar. He smiled eerily, a smile that made chills run down Edgar's spine. "Edgar, I thought it was about time I introduced myself. I'm Max. And this is Bill," he said, pointing to the muscular man by him.

Edgar extended his hand. "I know who you are. Nice to meet you," he said, as Max stared at Edgar's outstretched hand and laughed wickedly.

Max shook his hand and continued laughing. "You haven't made any friends in here yet, have you, Edgar?"

Edgar shrugged casually, not wanting to give any information away.

"What do you think about joining my group?"

Edgar hesitated as he immediately decided against it, but struggled to form the right words to refuse Max without being killed. Max noticed the pause. It was too long.

"Edgar, you're like us," Max said, clapping a hand roughly onto Edgar's shoulder. "You're going to be in here a long time. The rest of your life. You're still young. You still have a few good decades left. You should make the most of your time. Life is better when you have people who got your back. Don't you agree, guys?" Max said, looking at Tony and Bill sharply.

Tony and Bill both nodded in agreement with Max.

"See? So, what do you think? You in?" Max asked.

"What does it mean if I join your…group?" Edgar didn't know what would be expected of him. He wasn't sure what Max and his gang were up to in the prison. He didn't know if agreeing to join was the right move, especially because he suspected all of their activities were illegal.

"Ah, we participate in…extracurricular activities," Max said with a sinister grin, his white teeth gleaming. "You know, we play cards to pass the time, swap stories, you would always have us to sit with during meals. And most importantly, we got your back. But that means you got ours too."

Edgar stared at Max, unsure what the catch was. "That's it? Then what would you expect of me?"

Max's grin grew even bigger and more sinister, now looking similar to the Cheshire Cat's lopsided grin. "All I ask is that if I have a job for you, you do it, no questions asked. You have to do one small thing before you're officially in."

I knew it. But what choice do I have? Edgar thought. "Okay, what is it?"

"There's a guy in here who has been stealing our drugs and selling them. He needs to be taken care of," Max said, his smile vanishing, suddenly straight-faced.

"Whoa, what?" Edgar said, backing away from the three men. *I want no part of this. I'm not like Max and his friends. I'm better than that,* he tried to convince himself.

Max took a step closer to Edgar and continued inching forward. "Look, Edgar, I know what you did to end up here. You've killed almost as many people as I have. One more won't make a difference. You're already stuck here for life," he said with a sneer.

Edgar nervously ran his hand through his long dark hair. "I don't think so, Max. I killed because I had to, not because I wanted to."

Was it a lie? Maybe. But Edgar didn't consider himself the same as Max and his pathetic cronies. He never stalked women and he certainly didn't rape anyone. He would never do something so despicable. They weren't the same at all. People like Max didn't deserve to live.

Max stared coldly at Edgar. "I don't think you understand." Tony and Bill closed in on Edgar as if on cue. "I'm not asking you to do me a favor. I'm telling you what to do." Max moved closer to Edgar, so their faces were barely inches apart. "I've heard the rumors about you staring at the other guys in the shower. I understand; there aren't any women in here. Guys here are lonely and we all got urges. I can help you with that if you do this for me."

Edgar considered Max's offer. It didn't matter what Max promised him. He wasn't that desperate. He wasn't going to kill someone for a sexual favor. He shook his head slowly. He would never stoop to that level. He didn't need them. He was fine on his own.

"Sorry, not interested," Edgar said, turning and walking away from Max.

Tony grabbed him by the shoulder and dug in his long nails. "Where do you think you're going, bud?"

Edgar looked at the dirty fingernails gripping his shoulder in disgust. Weren't one of the guards going to do something? What did he have to do to make them pay attention and intervene?

Edgar thought quickly and slammed his head back into Tony's head, stunning Tony and making him tumble backwards into Max.

Max shouted, "What the fuck?" and angrily shoved Tony.

Poor Tony fell to the ground, dazed. Bill lunged toward Edgar as one of the guards finally looked over at them and noticed what was going on.

"Hey, stop it!" the guard yelled, inserting himself in between Edgar and Bill. "Go back to your cells now. Lunchtime is over."

Several more guards came over. One of them roughly pulled Tony to his feet. The prisoners were separated and escorted back to their cells.

When Edgar was safely locked in his cell again, he shakily breathed a sigh of relief. He thought about what Max asked him to do. Who did Max want him to kill? And why hadn't he asked Tony or Bill to do it if he trusted them? Now he would be on Max's shit list. For all he knew, he could be Max's next victim. He needed to be more careful. He couldn't afford to forget that he wasn't safe here. No one was looking out for him. No one cared what happened to him. He was alone. Edgar was more certain than before that he needed to escape if he wanted to survive.

Chapter 14: Delia

Against Joel's protests, Delia went to meet Carter, the first person who responded to her job posting. She agreed to meet him in a public place, a café, to minimize the risk. And of course, her Glock was safely tucked away in her purse. The safety was on, but it was loaded and ready to go. She wasn't happy about the idea of using it in a crowded café, so it was a last resort if Carter turned out to be crazy and attempted to hurt her. Her first response would be self-defense with hand-to-hand combat, which she also excelled at.

To her surprise, she entered the café to find that Carter was already there. He sat at a table near the back of the café with his resume on the table. He looked intently at his phone. He appeared muscular but slightly overweight. His black hair was gelled to the side and he wore a long-sleeve button-up shirt with khakis and black loafers. She assumed it was Carter, at least, although he looked incredibly young and she knew he didn't have the 10 years of experience she required.

Delia wondered if he had any investigative experience and if he was qualified for the position.

Delia approached the table and stopped in front of it. "Carter?" she asked hesitantly.

He jumped up from his seat and reached out his hand; his brown eyes were warm and inviting. "Yes! It's so nice to meet you, Delia."

They shook hands and both sat at the table. Carter had a half-finished cup of coffee sitting in front of him. Delia eyed the cup of coffee.

"Have you been waiting long?" She glanced at her phone to check the time. "We agreed to meet at 3:00 p.m." It was only 2:50 p.m. She assumed she would arrive before him and that she would be able to scope out the café, choose a table, order a drink, and prepare herself for the interview.

Carter bobbed his head vigorously. "I pride myself on always being early, especially for important things like this."

Delia smiled appreciatively. "That's great to hear, Carter. I see your resume sitting there. Do you mind if I look at it?"

"Of course. Although you'll notice right away that I don't have the decade of experience you asked for in the job posting. But what I lack in years of experience, I promise I'll make up for with my dedication, research, and thoroughness. I'm also trained in gun safety and have a concealed carry permit. I'm a quick learner and I want to learn from the best, which is why I was so interested in meeting you and applying for the job. I've heard all about what you did, your involvement with the Edgar Peterson case, and arresting him…" Carter rambled, but finally paused to take a breath and gulped down some of his coffee. "Sorry, I'm a little nervous."

"It's okay. And thank you for the compliment. I would prefer to hire someone with as much, if not more experience than I have though."

Carter's face fell in disappointment. "I understand." He picked up his coffee mug and sipped it slowly. "What if it was a sort of trial run? You could hire me and see how it goes for a while, like a 90-day probationary period. If you aren't satisfied with what I've accomplished by then, you can hire someone else."

Delia stared at him and he maintained eye contact. Carter seemed bright and eager. He was also direct and honest, all good traits for her potential partner. Sure, he was young, but maybe that would prove to be an asset? He hadn't been hardened by years of failed investigative work or seen terrible things that no one should have to see. Besides, she didn't have any other leads on a good applicant. She could at least give him a chance and if it didn't work out, she could resume the hiring process. Delia was also desperate to have someone to help her make sure Edgar was sentenced to life in prison for his crimes and, more importantly, to find Becca.

"Okay. We'll give it a shot. You'll have a 90-day trial period. If that goes well, then you're officially hired."

Carter grinned excitedly. "Thank you, Delia! I'm really looking forward to working with you. Like I said, I've been following the Edgar Peterson case since I heard about it last year. I'm excited to find out more about the types of cases we'll be working on together."

Delia took a deep breath and tried to remain calm. Edgar's name always filled her with anxiety. "It's an interesting case, alright. We'll go over the details of my current case next time we meet. How does Monday at 8:00 a.m. sound?" she hesitated, thinking about the fact that they couldn't discuss private investigative business in a public setting, especially regarding a case that most people knew about because it involved a serial killer who was also a famous actor. "I suppose we'll have to meet somewhere with some privacy, so no one can overhear us talking about the case. I'm currently, uh, in between places, so I'm living with friends and don't have an official office yet. What about meeting at the library? I'll call and book one of the private meeting rooms for Monday morning."

She typed the address of the local library into her phone and texted it to Carter. "There. Now you have the address."

"Sounds good, thanks. I'll bring a notebook so I can take notes and get up to speed on everything. I can't wait to learn more about the case we'll be working on," Carter said.

Delia smiled. "Great. I'll see you on Monday."

She rose from her chair and reached across the table to shake his hand again before leaving. He smiled warmly and squeezed her hand.

***

Delia did her best to prepare for the following week when she would be meeting with Carter for his first official day of work with her. She thought back to her first day as an NYC police officer—how young, excited, naïve, and full of hope she had been back then.

Delia entered the NYPD 19th Precinct. It was her first day. She knew she wouldn't be fighting crime her first day on the job, but she was excited nonetheless. She felt like a real police officer in her uniform and couldn't wait to make a difference in the world. This was what she was meant to do. Although, she knew initially it was up to her field training officer (FTO) to determine what type of policework she would be assigned. The FTO could put her on a multitude of tasks from arresting people who were drunk in public, reporting to a crime scene, or the location of an accident.

A middle-aged man accosted her as soon as she was in the building and startled her out of her excitement.

"Hey, honey, are you lost?" he asked with a salacious look on his face.

Delia smiled kindly, ignoring his comment. She survived the police academy and she was one of three women there, so she already had a taste of the sexism she would encounter throughout her career. But she was determined to have a good day. This asshole wasn't ruining it. And she would kick his ass if he tried anything. "No, it's my first day."

The man smirked. "A pretty young thing like you shouldn't be wasting her looks in this type of job. The police force is no place for a girl."

Delia rolled her eyes. She heard it all before. Or she thought she had. At that early point of her career, she had no clue the magnitude of the harassment and sexism she would face over the years as a female police officer, especially as a young, attractive woman.

"Make another comment and it might be your last day," Delia said, tossing her curly red hair over her shoulder, her green eyes shining dangerously. "I've had all the same training as everyone else and I was in the top of my class at the academy."

The man's eyes narrowed. "I was only trying to give you some friendly advice. No need to get all worked up about it." He walked away, leaving Delia sighing in exasperation.

It was only the first of many similar incidents. She wished she could go back to tell the 20-year-old Delia that she was tougher than she thought and that she would make it through everything. Maybe she was a little more broken now than when she first became a police officer, but she would make it out alive. And that was more than she could say about some of her fellow police officers who were killed on the job.

Delia knew the world was supposedly different now. Or better in some ways than when she was a young officer. But there was still a lot of change that needed to be implemented in the world, not only in policework, but especially in professions heavily dominated by men. Men like the one who made those rude comments to her on her first day on the police force, who were stuck on an ancient train of thought that women were less than men. As long as Carter wasn't a sexist pig or didn't try to make a move on her, she wouldn't have to worry about it. That was the good part about owning your own company and being able to hire the people you wanted to work with. There would be no room for misogynists at Wilson Investigative Services.

Delia finished setting up the assortment of breakfast foods on the table in the library meeting room. Delia had purchased a variety of pastries, scones, and a platter of fresh fruit, which was laid out on the table, along with a carafe of coffee. When she met Carter for the interview at the café, she noticed he ordered a mug of coffee and wanted to make sure he felt comfortable and had everything he needed for a good work environment. Hopefully it wouldn't be too weird working in a library meeting room. Delia wanted her own office eventually, but for now, this would have to work.

Carter knocked on the door and waved, startling Delia out of her reverie. She smoothed down her black skirt and stood to open the door for him. Her flouncy, lace maroon blouse with puff sleeves complemented her hair color. Her vibrant red hair fell in soft curls around her face. She had put on a touch of mascara to accent her green eyes. She didn't usually wear a lot of make-up, although she did take pride in her appearance.

Carter was holding two coffees in a travel container in one hand. His black hair was styled in the same manner as before. He wore a long-sleeve button-up shirt, this time a forest green color, with dark gray khakis. He had a notebook tucked under his arm and attempted to shift everything in his hands to awkwardly shake Delia's hand. She laughed lightheartedly and took one of the coffees from him.

"Hi, Carter. Thanks for the coffee." She stopped, not wanting to hurt his feelings, but also appreciating his thoughtfulness. "I'm not a fan of coffee, but that was nice of you to think of me."

Carter frowned. "Oh no, I'm sorry. I should have asked before I assumed you drank coffee. Of course, not everyone is as addicted as I am."

Delia waved off his apology. "Don't worry about it. It was a kind gesture. Although I did pick up a carafe of coffee for you this morning, so I *really* hope you like coffee…" she said, gesturing to the large carafe in the center of the table.

Carter snorted. "I guess I won't be running out for a refill today," he replied, following her into the room and setting down his belongings.

"I wasn't sure if you would eat breakfast before coming, so feel free to help yourself to the food whenever you're hungry."

"Thanks, Delia," Carter said, surveying the food and selecting a scone.

"We can eat first and then we'll dive in," Delia said, as she chose a chocolate chip scone and piled her plate with fruit.

She joined Carter at the table. "So have you always lived in New York?" Delia asked, making polite conversation as they ate breakfast together.

Carter shook his head, his mouth full of the scone he had taken a large bite from. "No, I grew up in a small town in Michigan. I always dreamed of visiting New York, so when I finally did, I ended up deciding to move here. I fell in love with the city right away."

"I've lived here my whole life, but I can't imagine living anywhere else," Delia said and took a bite of her scone. "Mmm, these scones are so good."

"They are. Thanks again for breakfast. If you like pastries and scones, I bet you would enjoy the patisserie on 5th Street. I go there with my girlfriend, Samantha, all the time."

Delia smiled. "That's nice, sounds like a good date spot. How long have you been together?"

"Two years," Carter said with a huge grin spreading across his face. He pulled out his cellphone and scrolled through it, then turned the phone so Delia could see it. "That's her."

The photo was a selfie taken of an absolutely gorgeous woman with sleek, straight brown hair to her waist, bright blue eyes, long dark lashes, tanned skin, and a light smattering of freckles across her face. The photo only showed her top half and she was wearing a form-fitting tank top that left little to the imagination.

"She's very pretty," Delia said honestly.

Carter looked at the photo again and put his phone away. "She is. She's also incredibly smart and witty. She's a lawyer."

"Well, should we begin? Are you ready?"

"Yup," Carter answered, opening the notebook he brought with him, his pen poised over a blank piece of paper. "So what case are you working on right now?"

"Our first case is…personal," Delia hesitated, not wanting to delve into all the specifics, but knowing that she had to if she wanted to save Becca.

"Oh?" Carter leaned toward her in eager anticipation. "What is it?"

"My best friend is missing."

Chapter 15: Edgar

Edgar had spent the last 24 hours terrified to leave his cell. He needed to decide what to do about Max and his gang. He assumed telling the guards wouldn't be helpful because they didn't intervene until a fight broke out. They wouldn't care if anything happened to Edgar. Besides, they let Max have the run of the place most of the time, which meant they weren't bothered by the illegal activities Max participated in from inside the prison. Whether he was selling drugs, committing violence, providing sexual favors, and apparently murdering people—Edgar didn't want to be involved.

James, one of the nicer guards, was currently stationed outside of Edgar's cell, vigilantly surveying the long hallway and ensuring he noted every person passing by, while still keeping an eye on Edgar.

"How's it going, Edgar?" James asked, walking by his cell for the dozenth time. He tended to pace back and forth for his entire shift. Edgar had the impression he wasn't the sort of man who did well with sitting still.

"Just trying to make it through another day, James," Edgar responded.

James grunted in agreement and continued pacing. He was a man of few words.

"Hey, what do you know about Max?" Edgar asked casually.

James stopped pacing and stood in front of Edgar's cell. "Max?"

"Yeah."

James cleared his throat and anxiously looked up and down the hallway, making sure no one was coming. "I'm only telling you this because I believe you're innocent and I think they made a mistake arresting you. Stay away from Max, Edgar. He's bad news. One of the worst people I've met in here. And I've met a lot of terrible people."

Edgar shivered imperceptibly, willing himself not to show his fear. "Okay. Right."

He wondered if he could trust James, if he could tell him the truth about what happened in the chow hall. Maybe it was worth it if one guard was on his side.

"You know what happened yesterday in the chow hall? Max asked me to do a favor for him, but it wasn't just any favor. He wanted me to—"

James cut him off. "I don't need to know what he asked you to do. I can guess that it wasn't good. Sorry that he's trying to rope you into his gang, but try to avoid him. If you become friends with him, you could get in trouble, and then screw up any chance you have of leaving here."

Edgar looked at James in surprise and wondered what he was implying. "What do you mean by 'leaving here'?"

James grimaced. "Innocent until proven guilty, right? You haven't received your sentence yet. You could still be acquitted. But be careful who you become friends with in here, Edgar. It could change the course of your life." His phone rang and he swiftly walked away to answer it out of earshot.

Edgar sat on the bed in his cell, contemplating his odd conversation with James. James had always been cordial to Edgar, but he wondered if James would help him escape. Was that what he was hinting at? Or did he really think Edgar's trial would go in his favor and he wouldn't be found guilty and sentenced to life in prison? Did James know something he didn't about the upcoming trial?

James returned much sooner than Edgar expected and banged his fist against the cell to gain Edgar's attention. "You have a visitor." He unlocked the cell, handcuffed Edgar's hands together, and led him to the visitor's center.

"Who?" Edgar asked in shock.

"David? He said he's your friend," James said.

Edgar smiled slightly for the first time in several days. Things were looking up if David had come back to visit him. He had been preoccupied with the altercation with Max and the certain punishment he would receive for his involvement, so he barely had time to think about anything else. Seeing his old friend would cheer him up. Even if he didn't remember him.

Edgar entered the visitor's center and spotted David waiting at a table for him. James brought him over to the table and stepped away.

"Enjoy your visit," James said, patting Edgar on the back.

Edgar cringed at the touch, taken aback. "Sorry," he said quickly. "I'm jumpy."

James' face reddened and he walked to the other side of the room to stand by several other guards in the visitor's center.

"Hello, Edgar," David greeted him.

Edgar waved in answer, waiting for David to explain why he was there. It had been weeks since he visited and Edgar was still suspicious about his intentions. His trial date had been set for September. It was the middle of July now. He was running out of time before he would receive his sentence. With each day that passed, his desperation to escape increased. But he still didn't understand what David wanted from him. What did David gain if he helped Edgar?

"Sorry it took me so long to visit again. I own a cabin near Asheville, North Carolina. It's a long trip here from Asheville."

"Wow, well I appreciate you coming all the way here again. I don't have any friends here or anyone to talk to, so it's nice to—"

David smiled warmly. "To talk about what?"

Edgar adjusted his glasses. "It's been a rough few weeks." He cleared his throat and lowered his voice, deciding trusting David was his best bet. "One of the gang leaders asked me to kill someone. I said no, of course, but now I'm a target. I'm not safe in here."

"Yikes. Sorry you're going through that on top of the trial coming up and everything."

Edgar finally stopped fidgeting with his glasses. "Yeah. So, what was our friendship like? I mean, you said we were young, but I don't remember anything."

David leaned back in his chair. "We went to preschool together. You were my first friend. I didn't have any siblings, but I always wanted a brother."

"That makes sense why I don't remember you then. I don't remember much from when I was that young. I'm an only child too," he lied.

He swore David's eyes darkened. "It sounds like your friend Jackson was a brother to you," David quipped.

Edgar's face flushed a deep red and he felt himself becoming hot. "Jackson was…my closest friend. The person I cared about the most," he said quietly. "Not a brother."

David's eyes sparkled with recognition, as if he understood what Edgar implied. "Ah, I see. Is that why you—"

"Why what?" Edgar cut him off angrily.

Jackson appeared in the visitor's center and hovered across the room, moving to their table, and floating next to Edgar. Edgar glanced at Jackson, noting that his decomposition was worse than before, but ignored him, despite the rotting stench and the grotesque bullet hole in his head.

"Never mind," David said, smiling good-naturedly. "It doesn't matter." He whispered, "It took me so long to visit again because I was formulating my plan. I had to make sure it was foolproof."

Edgar moved closer to David eagerly. He listened as David explained his plan to help Edgar escape from prison. It was risky and not foolproof at all as he promised, but it was the best chance Edgar had of living as a free man again.

"Don't trust him," Jackson said quietly, leaning so close to Edgar that he thought he would vomit.

"Why not?" he muttered under his breath.

"Even if he's telling the truth and you were childhood friends, why would he want to help you? Why did he wait all these years to contact you again? Think about it. He wants something from you. And I don't think it's anything good."

Edgar felt chills prickle on the back of his neck. Jackson had moved positions and was now floating directly behind Edgar. Edgar could no longer see him and didn't know what Jackson was thinking or why he was trying to get involved. He wanted him to leave.

When David finished talking about the plan, their visiting time was nearly up. He stood to leave and looked back at Edgar, questioning what he thought about his idea.

"Okay," Edgar agreed, looking at Jackson as he shook his head disapprovingly out of the corner of his eye. Tiny pieces of his flesh fell to the ground. "I'm in."

Chapter 16: Delia

Delia explained to Carter about how Becca had been kidnapped and she didn't have any leads about where Becca was or who took her. She was sure it involved Edgar somehow, but what friends or family members did he have left who could have implemented the kidnapping for him? His parents were dead, he didn't have any siblings, and as far as Delia knew, Edgar didn't have any friends either. The only real clues were the note and the doll. Delia had copied the note so she could reference it. She still didn't understand the name on the note. It must be a reference to whoever Edgar hired to take Becca, but she wasn't sure how it was connected.

The police officers she and Joel spoke to at the station had been nice, but it didn't seem like they were doing much to find Becca. In fact, they had brought Joel back in for questioning yesterday. They didn't have any leads and were going off the assumption that when a spouse goes missing, the husband is always involved. Joel was livid that they suspected him of kidnapping his beloved Becca and was intent on proving he was innocent.

It had been a week now since Becca went missing. Joel still wasn't working. He left the house early every morning and came home late every night. Delia didn't know what he was doing all day and hoped he wasn't doing anything to draw further suspicion to himself. He needed to get the police off his back and not give them a reason to think he kidnapped Becca. When he was at home, he was a shell of the Joel that Delia had known since they were teenagers. She knew the only way Joel would be okay would be if they found Becca. She only hoped Becca would be alive by the time they found her.

Delia sat at her desk in her bedroom staring at her laptop. The cases she cared the most about were the ones she couldn't solve. She wouldn't rest until they found Becca. NYC Police be damned. She would figure out where the hell Becca was.

Delia was startled out of her deep thinking by a knock on her bedroom door.

"Come in," Delia yelled.

Joel entered the room, hesitantly leaning against the doorframe. It was his house, but the guest room probably felt off-limits as long as Delia lived there.

"How are you?" he asked.

Delia shut her laptop apprehensively and stood from her chair. "Fine, what about you?"

Joel absentmindedly ran his hands through his hair. "I'm okay. I received a call for the hotline."

"You did? What did they say? Was it a lead?" Delia asked, anxiously cracking her knuckles.

"Yeah, it was an anonymous tip that someone resembling Becca was spotted in Maine. In downtown Portland."

"What? Maine?" Delia asked in surprise.

"At least we know where she is now. And she's still alive," Joel said, blinking as tears glistened in his eyes.

Delia shook her head in agitation. "I'm sorry, Joel, but hotline tips aren't always accurate." *Besides, why would Edgar bring Becca to Maine?* she wondered.

Joel gave Delia a puzzled look. "Then why did we set one up?"

Delia hesitated. She didn't want to tell Joel she suspected Edgar was involved with kidnapping Becca. She imagined the thought of his wife being kidnapped by a serial killer's accomplice wouldn't go over well. But she supposed it was time to tell him what she thought happened. She couldn't keep it from him any longer.

Delia inhaled slowly and released her breath. "Please don't panic, but I think Edgar somehow arranged Becca's kidnapping. He must have a friend or accomplice working for him from outside of prison and doing his dirty work. Whoever Ezra Bliftin is, they're connected to Edgar. The note was addressed to me, remember? I think the police are ignoring that."

Joel scratched the stubble on his chin. "I don't know, Delia. That doesn't make sense. If Edgar was trying to get back at you for arresting him, wouldn't he go after you? Did he even know Becca was your best friend?"

"I never told him about Becca, but there are ways he could have found out who I was close to. Social media, hiring a private investigator… Information like that is easy to find online nowadays," Delia said emphatically.

Joel straightened from his position leaning against the doorframe. "I don't think it was Edgar. I love Becca, but she isn't an angel. She could have pissed someone off. What if it was a psychotic fan who kidnapped her? The last few years she's become more well-known and she has readers who are obsessed with her books. Maybe it was one of them."

"No, I *know* it was Edgar—"

"How can you be sure of that, Delia? All we have is a note with a name that's probably fake, the creepy doll, and the anonymous tip that Becca was spotted in a city that has no correlation to Edgar."

"I know you don't want to believe Edgar's involved, but it was him. That's exactly the type of thing he would do," Delia insisted.

Joel crossed his arms over his chest. "Please don't take this the wrong way, but you've been obsessed with Edgar for so long that you might want to think he's the one who…you know… But that doesn't mean it was him. If you think about it more, then you'll see that I'm right. How could it have been Edgar? He's in a maximum-security prison halfway across the country. I doubt he's spending his time in there scheming ways to torture you. We know she's in Portland now. Can't you focus on the new information and find her?"

"Joel, I'm sorry if I'm being insensitive. I promise I want Becca home safely as much as you do. But it couldn't have been anyone else—"

Joel turned to leave the room. "Okay, Delia, I know how you are when you're convinced you're right. I don't want to argue with you *while my wife is missing*," he said angrily, exiting the room and shutting the door with more force than necessary.

Delia slumped onto her bed. Fighting with Joel was the last thing she wanted. She was supposed to be on his side. They both wanted the same thing: for Becca to be found alive. Maybe she should stop assuming Edgar was involved and start looking at other possibilities. She hadn't gotten anywhere with the Edgar theory yet, so she might as well try a new tactic. There was a chance Joel was right, after all. He wasn't a moron. Was she too close to the case because she cared about Becca? This was why she needed a partner she could trust to help her make decisions. Delia wasn't sure if she trusted Carter yet. They had only worked together for one day and she barely knew him. Carter knew all about her because of her brief stint in the spotlight with the Jackson Birkman case and arresting Edgar. But she needed help and Carter was all she had.

As Delia was contemplating everything, her phone buzzed on the nightstand. She glanced at it to see what the notification was for and swiped to unlock the phone and read the message. It was from the same phone number as before.

Delia, are you going to ignore my tip about coming to Portland? I'm making this so easy for you and you're blatantly ignoring my hints. Don't you want to find Becca? Maybe I should just kill her now.

Delia gasped and covered her mouth with her hand.

Delia decided she would talk to Carter about it tomorrow when they met at the library again. She could run the idea by him and see what he thought. It was better than continuing to obsess over Edgar if he wasn't a part of it. But even as she tried to convince herself to consider other possibilities, the thought kept creeping and nudging at the back of her mind, insisting she was right. Of course it was Edgar. It had to be him. Delia arrested him and ruined his life. If it hadn't been for her chasing him to Minnesota and hunting him down at his parents' house, he would still be a free man. Delia could only imagine how Edgar felt about her. The toxic anger building up inside of him, threatening to boil over. He already killed her friend Jerry. Now he had gone after Becca. She was sure that if she didn't stop him, Joel would be next. Delia knew the truth. Edgar didn't want to destroy her; he wanted to obliterate everyone in her life too.

Chapter 17: Edgar

Edgar couldn't escape directly after visiting with David. They had a plan and it involved being as careful as possible. He needed to wait a little bit longer, until the signal. It would be suspicious if he was able to break out after his friend visited. The guards and Minneapolis police would know David was involved. In the meantime, it was best to exercise caution. Edgar kept his head down, didn't interact with anyone in the chow hall, and stayed to himself when he was in the prison courtyard or anywhere outside of his cell. He did his best to avoid Max and his gang until he was free.

It went well for the first few days. On Tuesday, however, the day was off to a bad start for Edgar and he had a feeling things were going to get worse. The day started with the meanest guard on duty, the one who sent Edgar to solitary confinement for "disrespecting" him.

The guard stood outside of his cell, watching Edgar like a hawk. Edgar attempted to ignore him and read a book, but it was difficult to ignore someone when you could sense them intently staring at you.

"Hey!" the guard said abruptly, after 20 minutes of silence.

"Yes, sir?" Edgar said politely as he looked up from his book. He didn't want to push his luck with this guard. He didn't want to go back to solitary confinement.

The guard sneered. "*Yes, sir*," he mocked Edgar. "You're such a pansy. You need to toughen up."

Edgar swallowed and turned away from the guard, looking down at his book, but not really reading. *It's probably better if I ignore him. No matter what I say, he'll find something wrong with it, so he has an excuse to punish me.*

"You asshole," the guard spit, coming closer to the cell and pressing himself against the bars. "You ignoring me?"

"No, I—uh—" Edgar stuttered, caught off-guard. "I didn't mean any disrespect—"

"Disrespect? *Disrespect?* I can teach you a thing or two about that, you little bitch."

At that moment, one of the older guards walked by and the mean guard stopped harassing Edgar to greet him and chat for a bit. Edgar went back to reading, relieved that he was safe for the time being. No matter what he did, it was the wrong choice. He hoped David's plan worked and that he would be free soon, so he wouldn't have to worry about his safety every day. Although, he supposed he would have to be on the run if he managed to escape. He would need to significantly change his appearance and change his name. Almost everyone in the world knew his name and face now. If not from *Dispatching David*, then from his other exploits…

When it was time for lunch, Edgar sat by himself in the chow hall like usual, eating his lunch in his own little world. Sometimes Jackson joined him and sat across from him, but today he was alone. He hadn't seen Jackson since David's last visit.

A loud *thud* resounded on the table and Edgar looked up from his food, startled. It was Max, with Tony and Bill standing behind him protectively.

Edgar braced himself for the worst.

"Hello Edgar," Max said coldly.

"Fancy meeting you here," Tony said, chuckling.

Max rolled his eyes at Tony's dumb remark. "You got lucky last time when those guards intervened, but I don't give second chances. You've had plenty of time to think it through now, more time than I usually give people."

Edgar pushed his food tray away, no longer hungry. "I'm not interested," he said quietly, not making eye contact with any of the three men.

"Not interested? I thought I made it clear before, Edgar. I don't care if you're interested or not. If you want to survive, if you don't want me to kill you, then you've got to do this for me."

Edgar looked directly at Max, his eyes darkening as he felt the anger building inside of him, threatening to force its way out. He knew he was walking a dangerous line. Max thought he knew Edgar, but he had no clue what Edgar was capable of. He had tried his best to keep his head down and stay out of trouble, but Max was pushing him too far. "I'll only say it one more time. I'm not working for you. I'm not going to kill someone because you told me to. I don't need your protection in here."

Max's face was shocked, as if he couldn't believe someone dared to defy him. Then, he unexpectedly started laughing. "You've got balls, Edgar. I'll give you that much. You're a strange guy. Don't you at least want to know who I wanted you to kill before you refuse? For all you know, we might share a common enemy."

"No, I don't care who it was. I'm not a murderer."

At that, Max burst out laughing again, unable to control himself. "Okay, so you're insane. I know the evidence against you was overwhelming. We've all heard about what you did. Even if they can't prove you committed all those murders, they're going to nail you for enough of the deaths to make sure you're put away forever."

Edgar's eyes gleamed dangerously and Max backed away. "Leave me alone. I'm done talking to you," Edgar growled.

Max stood from the table and walked away, with Tony and Bill following after him. Edgar heard Tony ask incredulously, "You're going to take that attitude from that asshole, Max? You don't let anyone turn you down!"

Max snidely replied, "Shut the hell up, Tony."

Tony didn't say another word.

Edgar relaxed when the three men left, glad he apparently hadn't lost his threatening look. It was the look he perfected when he was an actor on *Dispatching David*. Those kinds of glares were fun to practice. Although Edgar had been absolutely terrified while confronting Max, he did his best to put on a show and act tough. They all thought he was a serial killer, so he might as well embrace the role, even if he didn't consider himself to be one. He did what he needed to for his own survival. He wasn't a cold-blooded killer like them. He was only an actor and he would play the role he had been given if it meant he could survive another day.

Chapter 18: Delia

Carter stared at Delia quizzically after she finished explaining why she thought Edgar was responsible for Becca's kidnapping. She needed to give him as much information about the case and the suspects as possible before delving into it.

"I'm not saying I don't believe you, but—"

Delia laughed harshly. "I can tell you don't. Well, it doesn't matter as long as we both examine every angle of the case and don't cross any suspects off the list yet."

"I agree. I don't think we have enough information to go after anyone."

Delia exhaled loudly. "You're right. Unfortunately, even if it was Edgar, we don't have any proof. But we do have a lead on where to look. What do you think about going to Portland, Maine?"

Delia showed Carter the text she received the night before.

Carter's eyes widened. "To look for Becca?"

"Yes, and to try to discover more clues. The anonymous tip and the texts are from Ezra Bliftin, but I'm still not sure who he is. I think going to Portland is our best bet, since we aren't getting anywhere in the case. Going to the last place Becca was supposedly seen is a step in the right direction," Delia explained reasonably.

"Good idea! I've never been to Maine before," Carter said thoughtfully, chewing on the end of his pencil.

"Me neither. This job will take you all over the country if it works out."

Carter laughed nervously. "How am I doing so far?" he asked.

"It's only been a few days, so it's hard to tell," Delia said honestly, regretting her word choice when Carter's face fell in disappointment.

"I'll try harder," he said in a determined tone. "I'll help you solve the case and find Becca."

"Thanks, Carter. I'm sorry if I'm being too tough on you. That's what it was like when I was a new police officer and I always wished I didn't have to work so hard to prove myself back then. I had to work twice as hard as the men to show that I was a capable police officer, and still, my hard work mostly went unnoticed."

"I'm sure it was difficult to deal with. It must be a lot better for you now being your own boss," Carter said with a small smile. "I hope I can prove that I'm the right partner for you. It's a dream come true working with you," he said, his eyes shining with admiration.

Delia blushed. "I appreciate the kind words, Carter. I hope it works out too. We should check out flights to Portland and try to head there as soon as possible. The flight's about 5 and a half hours," Delia said, pulling up Google Flights on her phone to browse the flight options.

But Carter was one step ahead of her. "I found a flight already," Carter said, turning his phone so Delia could approve of the flight. "Do you have a company credit card so we can book it?"

Delia swallowed nervously and grabbed her purse, pulling her company credit card out of her wallet. She thought about her small business loan from the bank and how this trip would entail spending another portion of the loan. Again, she wondered if the trip was worth the money, but decided it was. The business loan was enough to pay for a few months of business expenses, plus the salaries of herself and Carter. Thankfully, Carter hadn't expected an exorbitant salary and seemed excited to be working with her. Once the business took off and they had more cases to work on (preferably cases that paid them better), then she could give Carter a raise and put away some money in her savings account.

They were flying out the next morning, so they had the rest of the day to gather their supplies, pack, and prepare for the trip. Delia also needed to talk to Joel before she left. She felt bad that: 1. He would have to watch Lily while she was gone again. And 2. He was counting on her to find Becca, so if she failed, she would be failing him too.

Delia and Carter spent most of the day compiling their notes about the case, which mainly consisted of guesswork, since they knew so little about what happened to Becca or who took her. They knew the name Ezra Bliftin and the fact that they were somehow connected to Delia as well, since the note they left was addressed to her. There was also the matter of the texts being sent from Ezra Bliftin's phone and the tip they gave to the hotline. Besides those facts, they only knew that Becca was supposedly in downtown Portland, and it was one of the biggest cities in Maine. Delia also thought the tip could be a trap from the kidnapper to try to lure them to Portland and that Becca might not be there. They had their work cut out for them.

The task was daunting, but Delia couldn't give up on her best friend. She couldn't bring herself to sit back and let the police handle it. She had accepted complacency with the Jackson Birkman case and look how that turned out… A dead actor and several other innocent deaths caused by Edgar's hand. Her worst nightmare and her biggest regret.

***

Delia left the library because evening was approaching and she and Carter both needed to pack for their trip.

Joel was already home from wherever he was spending his days, sitting on the couch reading when Delia walked into the family room. Delia peeked at the book Joel was reading and recognized it as one of Becca's books. Her face softened. Joel was a good husband to Becca. He was her number one fan. He read all her books and supported her in any way he could. He encouraged Becca to quit the corporate job she hated years ago to pursue her true passion of writing books. It took many years for her to become successful, but it paid off. Becca was a mid-list author who earned a decent living from her books and had many loyal fans, which was every author's dream.

"Which book are you reading?" Delia asked, sitting next to Joel on the couch.

"Her first one," he said, closing the book and setting it down on the coffee table. "I thought I would re-read all her books and try to find any connections to Portland. If it was a psychotic fan that kidnapped her, maybe wherever they took her is a reference to one of her books."

Delia was surprised about Joel's thought process, but the idea was a good one. That is, if Edgar wasn't involved at all. "That's smart. Let me know if you find anything useful. I actually wanted to talk to you."

"Oh no, what is it now?" Joel asked worriedly. "I can't handle any more bad news."

"Nothing bad, I promise. Carter and I decided we should go to Portland to try to find any clues about Becca. Ideally, we could find Ezra Bliftin, but I'm not sure if that is likely."

Joel shook his head. "Delia, I don't know if that's a good idea. What if it's a trap and—"

"I can't sit by and let the police fuck up another case. Especially when it involves someone I love. With the Birkman case, I knew Edgar set up the murders, but I gave up too soon. I didn't do enough to prove it was him in the beginning. I need to prove without a shadow of a doubt who the culprit was this time, so I don't have to keep living full of regret and guilt. If I can find Becca and make sure she's safe, I won't feel like I've chosen the wrong career..." Delia said softly.

"Okay."

"Okay? That's it? You aren't going to argue with me anymore?" Delia asked, surprised that Joel seemed to be giving in so easily. That wasn't like him. They had many spirited arguments over the years, although they always made up in the end.

"No, it's a waste of time, especially if your time is better spent helping Becca. If that's something you think you can do, then of course I want you to go to Portland. But if you're going there, please bring her back. Please find her," Joel said and looked away from her, tears falling down his face for the dozenth time in recent weeks.

"I promise I'll find her, Joel," Delia said fiercely, instantly regretting her promise.

So many things could go wrong. She didn't know where to start looking for Becca. The city was huge, with more than 60,000 people, and they couldn't scour every inch of it or talk to every person. Delia shouldn't have promised Joel something so grand with so little to go on. But the promise was to herself as much as it was to Joel. She had to save Becca to save herself.

Chapter 19: Edgar

Edgar received the news as he ate dinner. A fisherman found Liam's body in a lake near Minnehaha Falls. Liam drowned months ago, so all that remained of him were his bones. A forensic pathologist identified Liam by his dental records. Now Edgar would be tried for Liam's murder as well. The fact that he told the police Liam left town to return to Lake Chapala, but no one had seen or heard from Liam in months was suspicious to the Minneapolis Police Department. Edgar was presumed to be the last person who saw Liam. The police knew they traveled together from Mexico to Minnesota. There was also the matter of the photo that was taken of them at the rooftop bar on their first official date. All that was left was for the police to prove it was Edgar who killed him. They were checking surveillance surrounding the area in Minneapolis to see if Edgar and Liam were spotted in the area together around the time they assumed he died.

The news filled Edgar with dread. He couldn't bear to think about Liam. He avoided thinking about him since the incident, but now images of Liam filled his mind. His handsome, concerned face when they first met in the restaurant in Lake Chapala. Their first date together. The countless nights they spent watching movies in Edgar's hotel room. Their road trip all the way from Lake Chapala to Minneapolis. Liam meeting Edgar's mom. Flash after flash of memory entered Edgar's mind until he felt dizzy and overwhelmed.

It wasn't his fault Liam was dead. He didn't want to think about that day, didn't want to remember what happened, but he couldn't stop himself from re-living every horrifying moment.

***

Liam stood near the flimsy fence at Minnehaha Falls, smiling broadly, waiting for Edgar to take a picture of him. Edgar moved to stand next to him and held his phone out, acting as if he was about to take a selfie. Suddenly, he dropped his phone, turned to Liam, and wrapped his arms around Liam's neck, in what Liam first interpreted as an overwhelmingly tight embrace. Edgar shoved Liam in the chest hard. Liam was caught off guard by the change in Edgar's attitude and stumbled backwards, his foot slipping off the edge of the cliff.

"Edgar!" he yelled in a terrified tone as he tried to scramble to safety. "Help me back up!"

Liam still didn't understand what was going on. Edgar grabbed Liam's hand and squeezed it one last time. Liam looked at him with relief, which quickly turned to a look of complete and utter betrayal as Edgar let go of his hand and shoved him again. Liam tumbled through the air, openmouthed, a horrified expression on his face as he awaited his fate.

***

Edgar shuddered. He couldn't stop himself from thinking about the condition Liam's body was discovered in. He hadn't been told the specifics, but his imagination was bad enough. He could picture Liam's attractive face eroded away by the water and time. He could have cracked his head open on a rock when he fell. Maybe that was why he drowned. Or maybe he hadn't been a strong enough swimmer.

Edgar could always say Liam fell into the waterfall, but he doubted anyone would believe him. It was too late for that. If Liam slipped and fell, then they would ask why Edgar hadn't reported it or called 911. Someone could have saved him. But he could still stretch the truth if it meant saving himself from being tried for another murder. He was already in enough trouble. All he could hope for was that no one discovered any pieces of his dad's body that he tried to dissolve with sulfuric acid, then chopped up and threw into the lake behind his parents' house. He didn't need the police discovering all of his secrets.

***

David was supposed to visit again to finalize the details of Edgar's great escape. Edgar felt on edge, anticipating meeting with David and breaking out of a maximum-security prison. It was enough to make any normal person feel anxious, let alone someone like Edgar. Edgar paced his cell for what was probably the hundredth time that day, going over all the possibilities in his mind. If he managed to escape without a guard or another inmate being alerted, then he was supposed to go with David to his cabin near Asheville, North Carolina. Apparently, the cabin was in a secluded part of the mountains and David said he rarely saw people. He didn't have any neighbors within view of his cabin. Since David told him he grew apart from his family and he didn't seem to have any close friends, he assured Edgar the cabin was a safe retreat until they figured out their next move. If everything went according to plan, then Edgar and David could stay at the cabin for a while.

However, if things went sideways, Edgar wasn't sure what he would do. He was in prison, so he didn't have any weapons he could bring with him while he tried to break out. If a guard attacked him, he wanted to be prepared, but he didn't have many options. He hoped that the intensive workouts he did daily for the last few months would be enough to help him if he needed to fight someone off. He hoped David would rescue him if he was in trouble. David looked tough, so between the two of them, Edgar thought they could manage to knock out any guards that tried to intervene.

Edgar couldn't concentrate on anything, so he continued pacing until a guard told him that David was there to see him. At last.

When Edgar sat down across from David at one of the tables in the visitor's center, he smiled upon making eye contact with him.

"David, it's great to see you again," Edgar said.

David nodded cordially and remained silent. His face looked strained.

Edgar's excitement wavered. Why wasn't David speaking? Was he not happy to see him? Was he having second thoughts about helping him escape? Was he going to back out and tell Edgar to forget about their plan? Edgar's throat threatened to close up in fear. He couldn't think about what he would do if David backed out. Not until he knew for sure what David was thinking.

"Are you okay?" Edgar asked, trying to breathe deeply and relax.

"Yeah, it's been an off day."

"Oh, sorry to hear that…" Edgar said unsurely. *An off day? Yeah, and I'm living in paradise here?*

David laughed abruptly. "Sorry, I realize that sounds like a shitty excuse when you're stuck in here. I don't know how much we have in common, but we used to be such good friends. I think that the more you learn about me, you'll discover we have similar…hobbies."

Edgar raised an eyebrow. "Hobbies?"

"Yeah, you know…" David said with a sinister smile. "How we spend our time."

Edgar snorted. "Okay then."

What if David wanted to team up with him? To be a partner in crime? Edgar already tried that once with Liam and that hadn't ended well. He didn't think he wanted to work with anyone again. He thought of himself as a lone wolf after he lost Jackson. He might be okay with having some sort of relationship with David. It would be nice to have someone in his life again, but he didn't want to get too close. Getting close to people was dangerous. That was why he killed Liam and his mom. Loving someone left you open to vulnerability and Edgar didn't want that. He preferred to work by himself. After all, two can only keep a secret if one of them is dead.

"Any questions?" David asked.

"What?" Edgar said, shaken out of his musings.

David leaned his head back exasperatedly. "You weren't listening, were you? I was going over the plan one last time."

"Oh. Right."

"Edgar, you still want to go through with this, don't you?" David asked quietly, ensuring no one would overhear their conversation. He crossed his arms over his chest in his leather jacket.

"Of course I do. It's a lot to think about and I'm feeling quite anxious."

"I understand, but I'm at risk here too. I hope you realize what a huge jump this is for me. If anyone finds out I'm involved, then I'll be joining you in prison. So, you better not screw it up," David snarled.

"You don't have to worry. It will be fine. I know the plan."

"Okay, then I'll see you tomorrow at the rendezvous point?" David asked, standing to leave.

"See you then," Edgar said.

David left and Edgar was escorted back to his cell for what he hoped would be one of the last times. He didn't think he would be able to sleep tonight. He was so wired and on edge, thinking about his great escape. He hadn't considered it much before, but he would be the first person to successfully break out of the maximum-security prison. He may not have achieved the level of fame and recognition he hoped for with his acting, but he would be remembered for something, and that was better than most people could say. Edgar didn't want to die and have his existence vanish completely, like he never existed. He wanted to leave a mark on the world and he didn't care if that mark was light or dark.

Chapter 20: Delia

The next afternoon, Delia and Carter landed in Portland, Maine. Their flight went smoothly and they arrived on time. They retrieved their checked luggage from the baggage claim and headed to the rental car terminal. After they checked into their hotel, they brought their luggage up to their separate hotel rooms.

When Delia bent to flash the keycard at the door to her hotel room, she noticed a sign pinned to her door. It was an envelope with DELIA scrawled on the outside. Her heart thudded in her chest. She glanced at Carter as he struggled to open the door to his hotel room. She swiftly unlocked the door to her own room and pushed her hand against the door to hold it open.

"Carter, come in my room for a minute."

He followed her inside and the door swung shut.

"Look what was taped to my door," Delia said, waving the envelope toward him.

"What is that?" he asked. "Did you open it?"

"Not yet," she said, ripping open the envelope and carefully sliding out a piece of paper.

Since you listened to my tip and decided to go to Portland, I thought we could continue the fun and games. I've always been a fan of scavenger hunts. Since you used to be a police officer, I bet you like them too. There's nothing like the thrill of the chase. If you win this one, then you'll find Becca. But if you don't, then I'll kill her. Good luck.

Clue #1:

There's a place I frequent in the city;

If you don't like to read, then that's a pity.

This store is full of fiction books of every kind,

Even the books created from Becca's mind.

If you're not incompetent and lazy,

Search for the first book about Daisy.

Ezra Bliftin

"Really? A scavenger hunt to find Becca? That's pretty sick," Carter said, his face turning whiter than usual.

"It is, but we have to do it."

"What does the note mean 'the first book about Daisy'?" Carter asked, re-reading the note.

"Ah, I get it. It's a reference to Becca's newest book series. *The Daisy Wilder Murder Mystery Series*. So, we need to find a bookstore that has the first book in the series in stock. Let's split up the list of bookstores and we can both start calling, so we finish faster."

"Okay," Carter replied.

Delia pulled out a notebook from her suitcase and scribbled down the bookstore's names, then split the list in half, passing one half to Carter. She walked to the other side of the hotel room and stood by the window as she dialed the first bookstore's phone number.

Of course the first bookstore didn't have the book in stock. Delia sighed in frustration as Carter hung up his phone and shook his head no.

There were over a dozen bookstores in the area. There had to be a better way to get through the list and not waste time calling each of them. Delia tapped her pen frustratedly against her notebook. She opened a new tab on her phone and searched for the book. The search results showed *The Daisy Wilder Murder Mystery Series: Book 1. In stock near you.*

"Yes! Found it."

Carter walked across the room to see what Delia was excitedly looking at on her phone. "Nice! So only two of the bookstores nearby have it. That's not so bad. We can check them both out."

"Yup, let's go."

Becca was a mid-list author, so Delia wasn't surprised that only two of the local bookstores carried her books. Becca's books had become more popular recently, but it wasn't as if she had achieved a Stephen King level of fame. Bookstores tended to be picky about the books they chose to stock and wouldn't stock books by unknown authors. Luckily for Delia and Carter, only having two stores to check out made things simpler.

Delia and Carter arrived in downtown Portland. It was a historic seacoast town full of restaurants, small businesses, and a gorgeous view of the water. There were a multitude of activities available—

lobster excursions, Maine beer tours, Henry Wadsworth Longfellow's childhood home, whale watching, and the Portland Museum of Art. It also happened to be the height of the tourist season, since it was July, so every street they walked down was packed with people exploring the city and enjoying their vacation. Delia wished she could enjoy the many wonderful attractions in Portland without wondering where her best friend was being held hostage and whether any of the people she passed in the street had information about Becca. She needed to stay focused on finding her friend and couldn't let herself get distracted by anything else.

"Where do you want to go first?" Carter asked, pulling out a map he snagged from the visitor's center. He perused the map, looking at all the restaurants and attractions listed on it.

Delia smiled lopsidedly at Carter. He was young and excited about being in Portland for the first time. It was hard not to find him adorable. It would be so easy to become distracted and sidetracked from their mission, but she was stronger than that. "I think we should go to the bookstore that's closer first and see if the second clue is there. If it's not, then we'll try the other bookstore. Afterwards, we can wander downtown for a bit, then we can grab an early dinner at one of the waterfront restaurants."

"Sounds good to me."

Delia and Carter explored the town together, with Carter holding the map and navigating so they could find their way around. Delia was a fine navigator, but she let Carter take the lead. She wanted him to feel like he was contributing to the case.

The duo walked several blocks before reaching the first bookstore. Delia headed toward the mystery section of the store, where she automatically perused the shelves looking for "Becca Morris." When she found a shelf in the Ms with Becca's books, she pulled out the first book in Becca's latest series: *The Daisy Wilder Murder Mystery Series*. She opened the book and found an envelope tucked inside.

"Is that the next clue?" Carter asked.

"I think so." Delia opened the envelope and pulled out a piece of paper. A message was scrawled on it:

Delia,

If you've made it this far, then congrats. You're one step closer to finding Becca, but she isn't safe yet.

Clue #2

The next clue is in a popular place,

One where people go to see creative works in a large space.

It's mostly inside, but outside there's a sculpture park

To wander if you arrive before dark.

Ezra Bliftin

Delia read the note over Carter's shoulder. "A sculpture park? I bet it's the art museum. I was looking up attractions in the area earlier and saw that they have a sculpture park outside."

Carter looked at the time on his phone. "It's after 9:00 p.m. now. They're probably closed."

Delia pulled up the museum's hours on her phone and sighed. Carter was right. "Okay, we'll go there first thing in the morning then. I hope Becca is okay. We didn't make it to the museum before dark like the note says."

"I'm sure she's fine. The kidnapper couldn't have known when we would arrive in Portland, so maybe they meant by tomorrow night. Or maybe they meant that the sculpture park is closed at night," Carter said.

"I hope you're right. We will go to the museum tomorrow and see where that leads us. We should also start asking business owners if they will put up a missing person poster with Becca's photo on it and keep an eye out for anything suspicious," Delia said.

A bookstore employee, a middle-aged woman with circular glasses and long black hair to her waist that was graying at the roots, wearing a conservative, long-sleeved purple dress with tiny white stars all over it, walked by them. "Anything I can help you find, dears?" she asked kindly.

"Actually, we were wondering if you could help us with something non-book related," Delia said, hastily shoving the envelope and note into her bag and pulling out one of the posters of Becca. "Could you please hang this near the entrance of your store and let us know if anyone has any information about her?"

"Oh my goodness," the bookstore employee replied as she read the information on the poster with a worried expression on her face. "Do you know her?"

Delia smiled sadly. "She's my best friend."

"Of course, of course. I'll hang the poster and let you know if I hear anything that could help," the woman said. "My name is Annie, by the way. I own the bookstore."

"I'm Delia and this is Carter," Delia said, gesturing to her partner. "We're in town investigating the case, since Becca was spotted here not too long ago. It's the only lead we have so far."

"I understand. Well, I wish you luck in your search. Be careful with whatever you uncover," Annie said, her eyes unexpectedly flashing with a hint of danger.

"Thanks," Carter said.

Delia and Carter exited the store and walked the several blocks back to their rental car with renewed energy about the case. Delia felt hopeful that they would figure out where Becca was. For the first time in weeks, she thought it seemed possible to solve the case. They could do this. They would find Becca before it was too late.

Chapter 21

I checked on Becca and left her alone in the room. My cellphone buzzed in my pocket, so I stepped outside for some privacy. I didn't want Becca to overhear any of my conversation. I nervously checked the caller ID.

"Mom? What do you want?" I asked, annoyed that she was calling me while I was busy.

Mom's voice came in a hushed tone, panicked. "Delia came to the bookstore. I think she found the clue in the store. I put the envelope in the book last night and it's gone now. She asked me to hang a missing person's poster of Becca."

"What? Did you hang the poster?"

"Well, of course I did! Don't get that attitude with me. I didn't want her to become suspicious if I refused. It's bad enough that I'm already covering your tracks for you."

I rolled my eyes, even though she couldn't see me. "Don't be so dramatic. It's your fault we're in this mess."

"How is this my fault?" Mom asked, outraged. "If it wasn't for your obsession with that silly girl—"

"Look, I have to go. I'm with Becca right now. I stepped outside for a minute, but I was about to start the next round of torture."

There was silence on the other end of the phone.

"Mom?"

"Yes, I'm still here," she said with a loud sigh. "Please be careful, honey. I don't want you to get in trouble."

"Don't worry, I'm being smart about it. I don't plan on getting caught."

"Oh, and one more thing. There was a young man with Delia in the bookstore. His name was Carter."

"Why was there a man with her? I thought she worked alone."

"I don't know. Maybe she has a boyfriend?" Mom suggested.

"Maybe," I replied, unsure that was the right explanation. "I have to go though."

"Okay. I love you."

I hung up without responding and slipped my phone back into my jean's pocket. Delia already found the second clue and there was a man with her. Was he working with her on the case? Did she have a new partner? Was he a police officer or private investigator? Why wasn't she by herself? The questions whirled through my mind as I struggled to regain control over my emotions. I didn't want to appear agitated in front of Becca. She needed to know I was in control. And so did Delia.

I headed into the room at the back where Becca was unconscious and handcuffed to a metal pole that ran horizontally along the wall. It was an abandoned factory and was as good a place as any to hold your archnemesis's best friend hostage.

The Long Shadow of Death

Chapter 22: Edgar

The only people who visited Edgar so far were Delia and David, unless his lawyer counted. Visits from Delia and his lawyer were not enjoyable, so unless it was David, he was sure the impending visit would ruin his day. The prison guard hadn't told him who it was this time, but he assumed it was one of them. Although he thought Delia would be back in NYC, so maybe it *was* someone else. He racked his mind to figure out who else would want to see him, but with his best friend and family dead, no one else came to mind. Maybe David wanted to see him one last time before his great escape.

The guard escorted Edgar into the visitor's center and brought him to one of the tables where a familiar looking, young, redheaded woman in her mid-twenties was sitting. She wore a black leather jacket, skinny jeans, and black combat boots. She looked agitated. She was Jackson's younger sister, Jessica.

He smiled as he joined her at the table and rested his handcuffed hands in front of him on top of the table. "Hello, Jessica," he greeted her with a small smile. He could only guess what she wanted from him. This would be an interesting visit.

"Edgar," she replied through gritted teeth.

"So, what brings you here?" he asked gaily. "Do you still live near Minneapolis?"

"I'm not going to tell you where I live. And I think you're smart enough to know why I'm here."

"Well, what took you so long to come see me?"

"Because I didn't believe it at first. You were his best friend," she replied, her voice changing to a much quieter tone.

Edgar did his best to steel himself for the conversation. "You didn't think I killed him?"

"How can you say it like that? So casually. Like you didn't tear him from this world, away from his family, friends, and his fiancée."

"I—I don't know. I haven't been convicted yet," he blurted out. Unexpectedly seeing Jackson's sister was throwing him off.

Jessica stared at him coldly. "Delia Wilson claimed you also killed Clara and made hers and Jackson's deaths look like a murder-suicide. I believe her. It makes a hell of a lot more sense than Clara killing Jackson. I know she would have never hurt him. Then, to make matters worse, you killed your mom. Your dad is missing, so you probably killed him too. And who knows if there were others!"

"I didn't kill my dad," Edgar muttered defensively. Just because he was the one who chopped him up, that didn't mean he was taking the blame for that one.

Jessica threw her hands up in the air. "So, you're admitting to the others then? God, I can't believe I ever liked you. I thought you were a good friend to Jackson, that you were a good influence on him. You seemed like you had your shit together. I always admired you, Edgar, but you were really good at keeping secrets, weren't you?"

Edgar smiled sheepishly. "I've been acting for a long time. I would like to think I'm a good actor. I became really good at pretending to be someone else."

"And it *was* all an act, right? You never cared about him. Otherwise, how could you do that to him?" Jessica asked, her eyes burning fiercely with something akin to hatred.

"No, you're wrong about that part. I loved him. That's why I had to do it. He was going to marry Clara and I knew it would all be over."

Jessica's eyes widened and she covered her mouth with her hand. "Edgar, Jackson loved you too. Maybe not in the same way you loved him," she added. "But he did love you. It wasn't enough for you though." She lowered her head and stared at the cold, metal table in between them. "Isn't it ironic that even though he was always the star, in the end, you're going to be the one who's remembered?"

"That's not all I care about," Edgar said angrily. "It wasn't about the show, or the fame, or recognition."

"You wanted Jackson all to yourself. You killed my brother so no one else could be with him," Jessica said matter-of-factly, as if she figured it all out.

Edgar's face blanched and he suddenly felt mildly nauseous. Jessica had known him for her entire life. She knew him better than most people left on this planet. He thought about what she said and pondered his actions, everything that happened between him and

Jackson, their relationship over the years, and how he ended Jackson's life. No matter how he tried to justify what he did, he knew Jessica was right.

Chapter 23: Edgar

This was it. The day Edgar had been waiting for. The day when he would finally be a free man again. Or as free as he could be as a wanted criminal. As soon as he knew he was safe, he would go after Delia. Thoughts of revenge threatened to consume him. He couldn't wait to kill her. Usually, he killed his victims quickly, but he wanted to make her suffer. Her death would be long and drawn out, until she begged him to kill her. Delia deserved to suffer like he did.

Edgar prepared himself for the escape, doing one last set of push-ups on the cold concrete floor. David wanted to slip him a pocketknife during their last visit. The guards always checked his pockets before and after a visit, so Edgar didn't think it was a good idea. But he also didn't think it was smart to try escaping without a weapon, so he planned to steal a shank from his cell neighbor. He had heard rumors about him making weapons and would make sure he escaped from his cell too, in exchange for helping Edgar.

Jackson appeared next to the cell bars, lounging casually against the door. "Are you sure you want to do this?" he asked, raising an eyebrow in concern.

"God, do you have to appear like that? You scared the shit out of me. And yes, I want to do this. I want the hell out of here," Edgar responded, annoyed.

"Do you trust David?"

"Y—yes. I do," Edgar stuttered.

Jackson laughed nastily. "You don't sound very sure of yourself. Is this the right decision? What if you get caught?"

"It doesn't matter. Nothing could be worse than being stuck in here."

"What if they kill you for trying to escape? You know the guards here aren't ethical. I bet they would make it look like an accident and no one would be the wiser. No one would come looking for you. It wouldn't be a great loss to anyone if you were gone."

"Well, thank you for that lovely sentiment, Jackson," Edgar muttered under his breath.

"I'm just saying—you have no clue what the consequences will be. Have you thought this through?" Jackson continued to pester him.

"I've thought about it plenty. This is what I want," Edgar insisted.

The light on Edgar's cell door flashed red, then a loud buzzing sound came from his cell door and all the others in his hall. He smiled and pulled open the door.

"Are you coming with me or not?" Edgar asked, turning to find Jackson in the darkness. He was gone.

Edgar shook his head. It was fine. He didn't need Jackson. He was used to being on his own. He quietly exited the cell, closing the door after he was in the hallway. He heard raucous noise coming from neighboring cells as chaos erupted. He decided it was smart to move quickly and stealthily toward the exit. He was sure other cell mates would realize their cells were unlocked and start escaping soon too. After all, it was part of the plan to cause as much chaos in the prison as possible. It would take all of the guards to handle something like this. Who knew how long it would take them to realize what happened? He only had a few minutes of safety to escape. David promised he would disconnect the back-up generators too, so it would take the guards and warden longer to make sure the power was turned back on.

Edgar swiftly opened the cell to the left of his. Surprisingly, it was empty. Well, that made it easier for him to obtain a shank. Now he could steal one and not have to worry about bartering or making a deal with another inmate. But where would he have kept illegal weapons in his cell? Edgar scoured the tiny cell as quickly as he could, trying not to disturb the inmate's belongings too much. Where could they be?

As he pulled books from the small shelf in the cell, pulled the thin blanket off the bed, and looked for any cracks or places that looked like a compartment or hiding place, Edgar became frustrated. He needed to find it fast. In one last attempt, he scanned the room again, wondering if a shank could fit inside the toilet. He bent to his knees and looked in the toilet. He thought he saw a flash of silver. Maybe metal? He carefully reached inside and pulled out a shank—a razorblade stuck in the end of a toothbrush. Edgar smirked and slid it into the sleeve of his shirt. Creative.

Edgar rushed down the hall, nearly bumping into James.

"Edgar?" James asked, squinting in the dimness. "Why are you out of your cell?"

Edgar panicked. James had always been kind to him and he didn't want to harm him. "Please keep walking and don't tell anyone you saw me."

"Why—what are you doing?" James asked in a concerned tone. "How did you leave your cell?"

Edgar sighed and pulled out the shank. He stepped closer to James and held the makeshift weapon to James' throat so he felt the blade pinprick his skin. James squirmed, but Edgar had his arm locked tightly around his neck and James was out of shape. He wasn't a match for Edgar.

"Edgar, please don't hurt me. You know I have a wife and kids," James pleaded. "I thought we were pals."

"I don't want to hurt you. Let me go and I won't have to do anything bad."

"Okay," James said. "What about a compromise? I can't in good conscience let you go without trying to stop you. I'll give you 15 minutes' head start. Is that enough?"

"Fine," Edgar said, releasing James and shoving him away. It would have to be enough.

James turned his back as if he hadn't seen Edgar and Edgar darted down the hallway. The exit door was within his grasp. He pulled the handle and turned the knob, breathing a sigh of relief as the normally secure, locked door, swung open. He wasn't safe yet though.

Edgar continued his path through the prison. There was another set of doors and a security checkpoint that he had to pass through before he could leave the building. He hoped the darkness, unlocked cells, escaped inmates, and power outage had left the guards frazzled, so he would remain unnoticed. He also hoped James would hold up his promise and give him a head start so he could make it out. He knew James was taking a huge risk in helping him. He would be fired if anyone found out that he saw Edgar and let him go without restraining him or bringing him back to his cell.

As Edgar opened the second set of doors, his heartbeat quickened. He was so close to getting out. The loud sounds coming from the cells were dimming the further away he went. He was sure that other prisoners escaped from their cells by now. He didn't blame them for trying to seize the opportunity for freedom. That was what he was doing. In fact, he hoped he wasn't the only who escaped. That would show them how flawed the security system was here.

He approached the security checkpoint and looked around cautiously. A bald, heavyset guard stood by the metal detector. He looked at Edgar as he walked closer.

"Hey! What are you doing out of your cell?" the guard demanded.

Edgar didn't bother responding. He was running out of time. He lunged forward with the shank in his hand and plunged it deep into the guard's neck. He stabbed him again, then a third time, relishing the feeling he had missed. The feeling of being in complete control. Watching someone's life force fade away. It was exhilarating and now that he had experienced it, he didn't think any amount of bloodshed would ever be enough.

He let go of the guard, who slumped to the floor, blood spurting out of his neck. Edgar's hands were covered in blood. He looked at them in fascination, wondering what the guard was feeling, wondering what it felt like to die.

The lights flickered back on, but they were dimmer than usual. The backup generator must have kicked in. Shit. Wasn't David supposed to disconnect all of them? Maybe a guard fixed them already? Edgar didn't have time to ruminate over what happened. Although only a matter of minutes passed since the cells unlocked, he wasn't moving fast enough. He needed to get the hell out of there. He nimbly stepped over the guard's limp body and through the metal detector. He sprinted down the remaining section of the hallway and pushed open the final door. He let the door slam shut, suddenly not caring about being quiet anymore. All he wanted was what he deserved—his freedom.

Edgar raced to the running car, a black sports car, parked outside the prison entrance. True to his word, David waited in the driver's seat. Edgar flung open the passenger's side door, threw himself into the seat, and buckled his seatbelt. David backed out of the parking space, spun the car around, and accelerated out of the parking lot.

As David drove, he turned briefly to look at Edgar. "So, you made it out okay," he said.

Edgar gave a thumbs-up, breathing heavily from fear and exhilaration. His blue scrubs-like pants and shirt were covered in sweat and his long dark hair felt drenched as well. He still clutched the shank and blood dripped down his hands.

"No issues then?"

"Nope," Edgar lied. It didn't seem pertinent to mention that James let him go or that he had been forced to kill one of the guards.

David was already an accomplice in aiding him with breaking out of prison. Why did it matter if there was a murder or two along the way?

Chapter 24: Delia

Delia and Carter ate breakfast in the hotel's restaurant the next morning, while they waited for the art museum to open for the day. Delia had already researched the exhibits in the museum and knew that the sculpture park outside was also extensive. But neither of them was sure where the next clue was hidden in the museum, so they thought it was best to split up once they were inside. If either of them found something, they would notify the other person. If the case didn't involve her best friend potentially being tortured or killed, Delia would have found the case quite fascinating. A scavenger hunt for clues; except if she didn't find the clues in time, what would happen to Becca? She shuddered as she tried to shake her thoughts away from the darkness.

"I know you think there's a possibility the kidnapper is tied to Edgar and I'm not saying that's impossible, but have you considered who else could be behind this?" Carter asked, munching on a bagel smeared with cream cheese.

Delia paused before responding and rested her chin in her hands. "I have thought about it, but there are dozens of people I have probably pissed off over the years working as a police officer. It could have been any of them."

Carter chewed his bagel thoughtfully, then swallowed before answering. "It was obviously someone who held a grudge against you. Enough to want to hurt your friend."

"Right. It's definitely personal."

"I think we're missing something."

"I think we should focus on the knowledge we have for now. We can go to the museum today and find the third clue, then hopefully find Becca," Delia said, her voice optimistic.

"We *will* find Becca," Carter said emphatically, as he looked directly at Delia.

"Thanks for all your help with this, Carter," Delia said, brushing several curly red strands of hair out of her face.

Carter's phone rang and he jumped up in excitement when he looked at it. "My girlfriend's calling. Sorry, I'll only be a minute!" He walked out of the hotel lounge and outside to talk to his girlfriend in private.

While Carter was gone, Delia tried to concentrate on finishing her breakfast. The sooner they arrived at the museum and began their search for the next clue, the better chance they had of finding Becca before whatever fate she awaited befell her.

***

Delia and Carter arrived at the Portland Museum of Art right when it opened, which wasn't until 10 a.m.

"Do you want to search the sculpture park or should I?" Carter asked unsurely.

Delia tucked her hair behind her ears. "I'll search out here and you start looking inside the museum."

"Okay, I'll call you if I find anything."

"We'll meet back here at 1:00 p.m. If we haven't found the clue by then, we can regroup and figure out our next move."

"Got it," Carter said.

Delia headed to the sculpture park. There was a large red sculpture of what looked like two waves, one on top of the other. There was a sign that clearly read, "NO CLIMBING ON SCULPTURES," but a small boy was clumsily climbing onto the lower wave. Delia watched who she presumed was his mom scramble to catch him before he fell. Families walked through the sculpture park, admiring the unique artwork, lounging on benches, and enjoying the sunny day.

She headed down the paved, red brick path and thought to herself, *follow the red brick road*, and wondered what she would find along the way. She only hoped it wouldn't be as disappointing as when Dorothy discovered the magnificent wizard was no more than a regular man behind a curtain. If Becca was killed, it would be much worse than that.

As she walked the path and examined sculpture after sculpture, each one stranger than the next, she began to think it was hopeless. Now the clue barely seemed like a clue and more like a taunt. It had seemed so simple since the location was obvious. But how were they supposed to find a clue in a place this expansive? It could be anywhere.

Delia saw an empty bench and sat down, deciding to rest for a few minutes so she could think. Her mind was preoccupied with Becca, and she pondered the first clue being discovered in Becca's book. The clue was tucked inside the first book in her newest series. The kidnapper put the clue there for a reason. Maybe she had been wrong all along. Joel, Carter, the NYC Police Department—they all doubted her insistence about Edgar's involvement. It was seeming more and more like the kidnapper was one of Becca's fans, someone who had become too obsessed with her and decided to kidnap her. Something about that theory felt off though because the note and clues were clearly left for Delia. If one of Becca's fans took her, then why did they want Delia to be the one to find her? Why did they bring her to Portland, of all places? And most importantly, what did they want?

After about an hour, Delia had thoroughly searched the entire sculpture park, so she headed inside the museum to continue the hunt. She browsed each room, trying to inspect the artwork cautiously, while being careful not to move too close. She didn't want to look suspicious and have one of the security guards ask what she was doing and escort her out of the museum. If she was still a police officer, she could have flashed her police badge and explained about the case. But she wasn't a police officer anymore. She was a private investigator and she needed to be creative about how she handled her cases now. That meant acting like a regular civilian and not drawing attention to herself when she was working on a dangerous case.

As 1:00 p.m. approached, Delia was nearly ready to give up. Maybe they could take a break and continue looking later. Their admission was valid for the entire day and the museum was open until 6:00 p.m.

Delia's phone rang and she swiped up to answer it. "Hey, did you find anything?" she asked when she saw that it was Carter who called, although she anticipated the answer was no.

"No," Carter replied. "Where are you?"

"Near the entrance. I'll meet you outside."

"Okay, I'll head that way now. See you soon."

Delia sighed in frustration and left the museum. She stood on the sidewalk, her back to the museum, squinting into the sunlight and waiting for Carter. She heard someone quickly approach her from behind and whipped around, unstrapping her gun from her holster in one swift motion. She expertly unlocked the safety and trained it on her assailant before they had time to react.

"Whoa, geez! It's me!" Carter exclaimed, backing away from Delia with a terrified look on his face.

Delia's face reddened to a shade even darker than her hair. She put the safety back on her gun and strapped it safely into the holster on her hip. "Sorry," she mumbled. "I thought someone was coming after me. I think being in Portland has made me on edge, since I know the kidnapper could be close."

Carter smiled nervously and approached her. "Well, you have really fast reflexes, so that's good to know."

Delia chuckled. "Yup, that's a result of years of being on the police force." She started walking down the museum steps, toward their rental car, and turned to look over her shoulder at Carter with a smirk. "Don't worry, you'll be as good as me someday."

Carter laughed good-naturedly and followed Delia to the car.

The Long Shadow of Death

Chapter 25

Becca whimpered in the corner of the room and adjusted her position to try to be more comfortable on the cool, concrete floor. The handcuffs didn't make it easy because there were only so many positions she could try with her hands locked to a pipe. Her hair was greasy from weeks of being unwashed and her outfit was covered in dirt and blood. Her face was smudged with what was probably a combination of blood and dirt as well. She was already falling to pieces and it had only been a few weeks since I kidnapped her. I thought she would last much longer before she broke down, but she had already begged me to kill her numerous times. She was so weak, so pitiful. *Based on the grisly stuff she writes about in her books, I expected her to be tougher...*

But I was still having fun with her. I didn't want the game to end yet. I enjoyed the thrill of wondering if Delia would find all the clues, if she would realize who kidnapped Becca, and if I would be caught.

The danger and risk of it all was terrifying and exhilarating at the same time.

I surveyed the museum earlier and spotted Delia and the man accompanying her searching the museum. I wanted to make sure I knew what was going on and knew which part of the scavenger hunt they were working on. However, when I checked the location of the third clue when the museum was about to close, it was still there. I stared at in disbelief. They didn't find the third clue. That meant Becca was mine for a little bit longer. Maybe Delia wouldn't find the next clue. I panicked when she found the first two clues so quickly and worried that it would be over too fast, but now she didn't seem as smart as I thought.

I smiled to myself. *Good, then I don't have to worry about the game ending yet. Becca is all mine still. Let the fun and games continue…*

Chapter 26: Edgar

David drove like a madman, speeding until they were nearly an hour away from the prison. It made Edgar nervous because he worried David would be pulled over by the police for driving over the speed limit. If that happened, then the police would see him and realize who he was. Edgar assumed every police officer and law enforcement official in the country knew what he looked like. He would be screwed if they were pulled over. He would be dragged back to prison and punished for breaking out. Placed in solitary confinement indefinitely. Or maybe they would find a way to enact the death penalty on him, even though it wasn't legal in Minnesota. Or one of the inmates could kill him and make it look like an accident.

"Edgar, stop worrying. You're free," David said, guessing what Edgar was stressed about and glancing at him as he drove.

Edgar looked down at his hand. He was tightly clenching the console, his bloodied fingernails digging into the leather. He released his hand from the console and turned to look out the window. "I don't think I'll ever stop worrying."

"I didn't help you escape, so you could live the rest of your life in fear. You're the first person to escape from Harriet Heights Maximum Security Prison. You're going to be a legend!" David said, smiling broadly.

The corners of Edgar's lips turned up, despite the fact that he was still terrified of the consequences. "It will be pretty awesome."

"Of course, you'll still have to be careful for a while until we know they can't find us."

"So how exactly did you do it? You never told me all the details."

"Ah, yes, my brilliant plan. It took so long because I had to find someone to hack into the prison's computer system. After a bit of research about prison security and the locks on the cell doors, I discovered that most modern-day prisons operate almost exclusively electronically. That means the cell doors can all be locked or unlocked through a computer system. It also means the system can be hacked." David smirked at the look on Edgar's face.

"You hired someone to hack into the computer system then?" Edgar asked.

"Not quite. After looking at the public record for the prison employees, I found out who oversees the prison's computer system. I tried asking him nicely to hack into the system and disable all the locks. At first, he refused. Then, I threatened to kill his wife and kids. He did everything I said after that."

"What? But if he saw your face and knows you helped me escape, then he's going to turn us in!" Edgar exclaimed worriedly.

"Don't worry, I took care of him."

"You mean—"

"There's nothing to worry about, Edgar. I promised I would help you and I took care of everything."

"Do you think they'll suspect right away that you were involved in my escape?" Edgar asked ruefully. "Can't they figure out where your cabin is and track us down?" he wondered, panicking that this had all been a terrible mistake. What had he been thinking trusting someone he barely knew with his freedom and his life?

David shook his head and tapped his fingers on the steering wheel to the beat of the classic rock music playing on the radio. "Nope. They don't know my legal name. I was adopted as a baby and my adopted parents changed my name. All that stuff was kept quiet in the adoption because my birth mom didn't want anyone to find out."

"You were adopted?" Edgar asked, scrunching his eyebrows together. "Were you already living with your adopted parents when we became friends then?"

David peered at him out of the corner of his eye, but stayed focused on driving. "You still don't trust me, do you?" he asked, ignoring Edgar's questions.

"I'm sorry. I don't trust people very easily and after everything that's happened—"

"It's okay. I'm not sure yet if I trust you either," David said.

Edgar laughed uneasily. "I guess we both need to work on that then."

"Well, we'll have plenty of time. The drive is going to take 17 hours, plus extra time to stop for gas, food, and to use the bathroom. I think we can do it in about two days. When we're halfway, we can find a motel. Probably somewhere in Illinois or Indiana."

"Sounds good to me. Sorry I can't help you out with the driving. I'll need a fake ID if I want to be able to drive and buy a car, rent an apartment, or buy alcohol," Edgar mused, thinking about all the things he would need to do to ensure he wasn't found by the police, some other type of law enforcement, or Delia. He liked the prospect of Delia finding him because it meant he would have another chance to kill her. "Although, I need to change, clean up, and somehow disguise my appearance in the meantime. People will recognize me. I can't stop anywhere looking like this."

"I was thinking that too. Your face is already recognizable from *Dispatching David*, but as soon as the guards at the prison realize you escaped, your face will be plastered all over the news and the Internet. If it isn't already. There's a hat and a change of clothes in the backseat. That will help a bit if people aren't too close to you."

"Good point. When we stop, can we go somewhere that has scissors and hair dye?"

David laughed obnoxiously. "Sure. What color are you going to dye your hair?"

Edgar pursed his lips unhappily as he contemplated his options. "I don't know. Nothing crazy. I never wanted to dye it for any acting gigs or auditions, so I don't relish the thought of changing my appearance, but I don't have a choice. A lighter brown, maybe?"

"If you chop off enough of your hair, you'll look like a different person anyways." David attempted to comfort him.

"Yeah, it's become a bit unruly the last few months," Edgar said, self-consciously pulling at the split ends on his long, stringy dark hair.

Their road trip halfway across the country continued with minimal hiccups. No one seemed to be following them and police officers or law enforcement hadn't stopped them. They even listened to the news on the radio, but there wasn't any mention of Edgar's escape yet. It seemed like the two men were going to make it to North Carolina without any major issues. Maybe they would bond along the way. And most importantly, Edgar was going to be safe. Or so he thought.

Chapter 27: Delia

Delia and Carter wandered the town for a while, then grabbed a late lunch at a seaside café. After lunch, they decided to head back to the museum and try searching for the clue again. There were still a few hours until the museum closed. They might be able to find the third clue before then.

When they arrived at the museum, they split up like before, each private investigator scouring the museum for anything out of the ordinary. They both tried their best to carefully examine any areas or pieces of artwork that they might have overlooked the first time. Delia was in a room she visited previously when she spotted an Andy Warhol painting she hadn't paid attention to before. Nothing in particular about the painting stood out to her, besides the bright colors, but upon a second glance she noticed a note on the bottom right corner of the painting. There was a thumbtack in the top right corner of the note, pinning it to the painting. All the note said was "Delia" and there was a QR code below her name.

Was the third clue seriously on a priceless painting? A note that anyone could have grabbed or scanned with their phone? Or it could have fallen off and been lost forever? How long had the note stayed there unnoticed? Didn't any of the guards or security check the paintings and artwork for anything suspicious? Delia's mind raced as she wondered how stupid the person was who had taken Becca. *Pretty stupid*, she assumed, *if they left a clue on an expensive painting in a popular museum in Portland.*

She took out her phone and snapped a quick picture of the QR code on the note. She tried not to panic over the fact that she would be recorded on the museum's security cameras standing in front of the painting and taking a photo, and hastily stepped out of the room.

She texted Carter:

Meet me at the entrance. I found the next clue.

Delia left the museum for the second time that day. She waited until Carter joined her outside to see what the QR code from the photo would reveal on her phone. At least the kidnapper hadn't been stupid enough to put the clue out in the open for everyone to see.

Clue #3:

2 clues left. You're getting closer.

Grab a coffee on 51st Street and mull things over.

But you should be sure of your next route.

Will you find Becca before her time runs out?

Ezra Bliftin

"A coffee shop on 51st Street?" Carter said, looking at the time on his phone. "We could head there now. It's still early."

"Absolutely, let's go."

They went back to their rental car and Delia drove them to 51st Street. She parallel parked expertly across from a boutique clothing store and turned off the car. She looked over at Carter, who had been Googling "coffee shops on 51st Street in Portland, Maine."

"Well, there are two coffee shops on this street. One has wine, liquor, and food too, but the other one only serves coffee. Which one should we try first?"

Delia anxiously twirled her hair around her finger. "The one with wine and liquor. The clue says to 'mull things over,' which I'm assuming is a wine reference."

Carter opened the passenger door, but Delia placed her hand on his shoulder to stop him before he exited the car.

"Wait, I know we don't want to go to the police about this since they haven't been any help, but we should at least make sure all the clues are safe. They will be evidence."

"Right. I'll put them in the glove compartment and then after we find Becca, we can go to the police and tell them everything," Carter said.

Delia followed Carter as he navigated to the coffee shop. It was called "Brewed to Death," which seemed fitting given the situation. Apparently, it was a specialty coffee shop, where they roasted, ground, and brewed their own beans in house. It made sense to Delia that they sold alcohol too, so they had a reason to stay open later and draw in customers. Not everyone liked to drink coffee, especially later in the day.

They entered the coffee shop with trepidation, neither of them knowing what to expect. The coffee shop was small and cozy; the smell of freshly ground beans permeated the air. Witty coffee-related sayings were hung in frames on the wall. "Coffee and friends make the perfect blend," "espresso yourself," and "I have measured out my life with coffee spoons," which Delia recognized as a famous quote by T.S. Eliot. Several plush couches and armchairs were scattered throughout the space, as well as a few tiny tables with two chairs at each table. She estimated that about a dozen people could be seated inside at a time, which meant most people grabbed their coffee to go.

Carter stepped up to the counter and Delia followed him.

"What are you doing?" she whispered anxiously to him.

He looked at her, bewildered. "Ordering a coffee."

"Oh. Right," she responded, embarrassed that she assumed he was going to ask the barista about the clue. She still didn't want to draw any attention.

Carter ordered their "coffee of the day," which was one of their specialties. Delia knew he didn't consider himself a coffee connoisseur, but she didn't even like coffee, so she knew less than he did about the caffeinated beverage. Delia scanned the menu and ordered a hot chocolate.

When they grabbed their drinks from the pick-up counter, they found an empty couch and sat next to each other to think about what to do next. The coffee shop was so small that anything they did would be noticed by the employees and most likely by the other customers as well. They needed to be careful. Carter sipped his coffee and Delia surreptitiously looked around the space.

There was a man of average height whose face was obscured sitting in one of the armchairs diagonally across from Delia and Carter. He wore a baggy, dark blue and white striped hoodie zipped up all the way and a plain baseball cap with wavy blond hair spilling out of it. He was the only other customer in the coffee shop. Delia noticed him glance over at them multiple times and made eye contact with him after the first few times. She was caught off guard by his striking blue eyes, which seemed oddly familiar. *Is he the man leaving the clues, the one who took Becca? Ezra Bliftin? Who is he?*

Delia had the information from all the clues saved on her phone, so she went through them again as she contemplated the name. Ezra Bliftin. She had already considered the fact that it was a fake name, so the kidnapper could remain anonymous, but for the first time she wondered, what if it was an anagram? What if their identity had been hidden in plain sight from the beginning?

Carter looked at her phone as she worked to rearrange the letters in the name. She whispered to Carter that he should look for the fourth clue while she continued her word scramble. After a few more minutes of trying to figure out the real name, she wondered if it really was an anagram or if she was wasting her time. A stack of magazines was scattered haphazardly across the coffee table in front of her. She idly glanced at them, but the name on the corner of one of them piqued her interest.

Clara Rogers. Jackson's fiancée. That couldn't be a coincidence, could it? She slid the magazine out of the stack and looked at the front cover. It was an older issue of *Women in Style* from the winter, shortly after Jackson and Clara died. Delia thought it was odd that Clara was on the front cover, so she opened the magazine and scanned the table of contents inside to find the article about Clara. She knew Clara had been an editor at a women's magazine, but had forgotten that *Women in Style* was where she worked.

On the first page of the article about Clara, which served as a tribute to the former magazine's editor, there was a note that said "Delia" with another QR code. The fourth clue. Without bothering to think too much about it, Delia scanned the QR code on her phone. She spotted Carter a few tables over and made eye contact with him as the man in the blue-striped hoodie hopped up from his seat.

She gave a slight nod to Carter, who discreetly patted his gun in his jacket pocket, making sure it was still there.

Their original mission was to find clue #4, but had they stumbled into a trap? Were the clues all a set-up for some larger scheme? Was the blue-striped hoodie guy the one who kidnapped Becca? Or was he a local police officer? He was wearing regular clothes and didn't look like a typical police officer, but Delia was never judgmental about that sort of thing. After all, most people found it hard to believe that she was a former police officer so she didn't like to make assumptions.

Carter returned to the couch, set his coffee down on the dark, rectangular wooden table in front of them, and leaned in close to her. His lips were inches from her ear as he whispered, "Is that guy here for us?" His breath smelled like the coffee he had finished moments ago.

Delia leaned into Carter, resting her head on his shoulder. "I think so. Play along," she whispered.

Carter swallowed and nodded. His right hand was clutching the arm of the couch and his nails were digging into the fabric. He seemed nervous. Was it because they didn't know what type of situation they were involved in yet and they could be in danger? Or was it because—

Her confused thoughts were interrupted by the blue-striped hoodie guy as he walked hurriedly to the door.

"Should we go after him?" Carter asked quietly, putting his arm around Delia.

"Yeah, let's see where this guy is going."

Carter stood, grabbed his coffee in one hand, and extended his other hand to Delia. She smiled at him and placed her hand in his. They walked out of the coffees hop hand-in-hand toward their fate.

As they exited the coffees hop, they spotted the blue-striped hoodie guy around the corner, walking toward a beaten up-looking white sedan. He held his phone to his ear.

"Yeah, they were in the coffee shop," they heard him say to the person on the other end of the phone.

"No, I don't think they found the fourth clue yet." He snorted. "Right." Pause. "Nah, I think he's her boyfriend or boy toy."

Delia rolled her eyes. Blue-striped hoodie guy looked up and down the street as he opened his car door and spotted them staring at him.

"Shit!" he exclaimed, fumbling with his phone and nearly dropping it. "Gotta go, Mom," he said, quickly hanging up the phone and jumping into the driver's seat of the white sedan.

But he was too slow. Delia and Carter were already quickly approaching his car, with Carter making it to the car as the man was putting the car into reverse. Carter ran track in high school and still enjoyed running, so he was quicker than Delia, although she was in shape.

"Where do you think you're going?" Carter said, stepping up to the car's window.

The man panicked and continued trying to back out of the spot where he parallel parked, but he was either too nervous or an inexperienced driver, so he ended up in the exact spot where he started in the parking space.

Carter laughed as he watched the man struggling and turned to Delia, shaking his head in amazement. He reached into the driver's side window, which was partially rolled down, and grabbed the man's arm. "Turn off the car," he said calmly.

At this point, Delia caught up to Carter and the blue-striped hoodie guy and dangled her loaded gun casually in her right hand. "Sir, please step out of the vehicle."

The man tried to roll up the window, but it seemed to be stuck and wouldn't close. He groaned and turned off the engine, slowly making his way out of the car. He brandished his own gun in his hand.

Armed and dangerous, Delia thought. *We need to be careful because we don't know what he's capable of. If only Carter and I had time to plan our ambush...*

"What do you want?" the man asked, standing outside his car and looking back and forth between Delia and Carter. He seemed surprisingly nervous.

"You were watching us in the coffee shop," Delia started, trying to approach the situation calmly and not accuse him of anything before she knew the truth. He might not be involved with the kidnapping. It could all be a coincidence. Maybe he was a creep who stared at her because he found her attractive. Or someone who recognized her from working on the Birkman case. "Why were you in the coffee shop?" she asked.

The man laughed harshly. "I know who you are, Delia," he answered, ignoring her question. "You're famous for being involved in the arrest of the famous actor, Edgar Peterson." He jerked his head to Carter. "No idea who that guy is though."

"I'm her partner," Carter said coldly.

"Hmm, okay," the man replied, appraising Carter. "You look kind of young to be with someone that old, but who am I to judge?"

Delia's face reddened intensely at the implication. *I'm only 34!* She thought, annoyed that this random man called her old. As if she wasn't insulted enough in her field. She tried to regain her composure quickly. They were supposed to be catching him off guard, not the other way around.

Carter burst out laughing in a series of loud puffs of air, nearly doubled over with the effort. "You think *she's* old? How old are you?"

Blue-striped hoodie guy rolled his eyes and gripped his gun tightly in his hand. "Let's not stray off topic here. Why are you two following me?"

Carter's eyes narrowed. "You were following us first."

"Okay, okay," Delia interjected. "It doesn't matter who was following who." She paused, pursing her lips, her hands on her hips, exuding intimidation. "Who are you?"

"I would be pretty stupid if I answered that," the man said with a sneer.

Delia sighed exasperatedly, not that she had assumed this would be easy. She wanted to scream at him to tell her where Becca was. Although she had been wrong about Edgar being involved in Becca's kidnapping, so maybe she was wrong about this guy too?

"Are you the one who left the clues?" Delia asked. "Becca's office, the bookstore, the museum, the coffee shop…"

The man tilted his head to the side, bemused with her. "You never found the last clue," he said with confidence.

"How do you know that?" Carter sputtered.

"She didn't say the location of the last clue when she listed where the first, second, third, and fourth clues were," the man said, stating the obvious. "Otherwise, why would she have left it out?"

Carter groaned and Delia shot him a look, as if warning him to quiet down. He looked back at her embarrassed and refrained from saying anything.

"Well, it's been nice chatting with you both, but I've got things to do, people to kill… I mean, torture—"

"That's not funny," Delia replied, her eyes glinting with anger. She didn't have time to call the police or worry about going through the proper channels for arrest. She needed answers. "And I don't think you're going anywhere," she said, charging forward and tackling him to the ground.

As she tackled the man, the hood of his hoodie came off, revealing all of his messy, wavy blond hair and the full impact of his sparkling blue eyes. And then Delia realized how she knew him.

Chapter 28: Edgar

After the last stop on their road trip, Edgar's hair was dyed a honey brown color. He pulled his hair into a ponytail and asked David to chop it off. Edgar wasn't happy with his appearance now, but it would do for the time being. He could always see a hair stylist and have them fix his hair and style it more attractively for him. Then again, did it matter if he looked good anymore? It's not like he was trying to pick up guys. *Those days are probably over*, he thought sadly, as he imagined his future alone.

As they approached North Carolina, Edgar didn't know his childhood friend any better than he did before embarking on a road trip with him. He still didn't trust him and wondered how he could manage to find out if they really knew each other as kids. He certainly couldn't ask his parents if they remembered David, considering they were both dead.

Edgar was also unsure about what to expect when they finally reached David's house. David told him there were two bedrooms and two bathrooms, so at least he would have his own private space. But he didn't have any personal belongings with him, other than the few items he had been allowed to keep with him in prison. A photo of Jackson. A worn paperback of Edgar Allan Poe's short stories that had been a gift from his parents. He couldn't bring himself to part with it, even after the chilling secrets his mom revealed to him shortly before her death.

He would need to buy clothes. He borrowed a hat and an outfit from David, so he didn't look conspicuous in his prison inmate's uniform walking around at rest stops and gas stations. Edgar almost chuckled to himself as he imagined passersby's reactions to seeing a prison inmate in the outside world. They would be struck with fear, especially if they recognized him. Edgar liked the thought of people fearing him. It was too bad he couldn't let anyone find out who he was.

He had seen the barely concealed looks of terror on the prison guard's faces and the way most of the inmates avoided him. They all thought of him as a serial killer. And he hadn't thought of himself as one until recently, after Liam's body was discovered, and he realized how many people he killed. He supposed the term was accurate, even if he wasn't happy about it.

"What are you grinning at?" David asked, looking over at him with a bemused expression on his face.

"Ah, just thinking," Edgar replied with a light chuckle. He turned to look out the window and rested his head in his hand.

"Only a few hours left until we arrive at my place."

Edgar responded with a slight nod. He wasn't in the mood to talk. In fact, he wondered how he would handle living with David. It had been years since he lived with someone else. The last person he lived with was Jackson, when he first moved to NYC. Jackson was the only roommate he hadn't minded, but he didn't want to think about those days. Back when he and Jackson were inseparable. Before he met Clara.

Even in prison, he had his own cell. *Nothing can be worse than prison,* he tried to assure himself.

***

They pulled up in front of a log cabin. David had been right about the location, at least. It was in the middle of nowhere, with no neighbors within a mile on either side. The cabin was nestled in the Great Smoky Mountains, which were true to their name. Edgar could barely see the mountains in the distance because of the thick smoke-like clouds that hung heavy in the air, obscuring the view. Edgar was also surprised to see a garden in the front yard of the cabin. David hadn't struck him as a gardener, but he supposed he didn't know much about him yet.

"Well, this is it. Let me show you around," David said, getting out of the car and gesturing for Edgar to follow him.

Edgar walked toward the cabin behind David and tentatively entered the house. It was homey, decorated to fit the mountain, woodsy vibe. Landscape portraits were hung on the walls. The furniture was simple and looked like handcrafted wood. The small sitting room and kitchen seemed to be mostly decorated in neutral colors. The sitting room was filled with two oversized armchairs, a coffee table, and a fireplace took up an entire wall. The kitchen had appliances that looked slightly outdated, white cabinets, and a square table against one wall with two wooden, black chairs on either side of it. The kitchen table overlooked a large window which revealed a view of the mountains.

"Come on, I'll show you the bedrooms. The bigger one is mine, but the spare bedroom isn't too bad," David said, walking to the first door. "This one is mine."

"Nice," Edgar said, unsure what he was supposed to say and not wanting to be rude because of his friend's kindness and all the help he gave him so far.

The truth was nothing about the place was nice, or at least not in the way Edgar thought of things as nice. But he knew he should be grateful for everything David did for him. Although in his former life, Edgar had been a moderately successful, wealthy actor, prison made him appreciate the finer things in life he had been used to even more. So, this cabin wasn't really his style, but it would be fine. Besides, he didn't have to stay here forever. Maybe he and David wouldn't get along and they would part ways. Edgar survived on his own before and he could do it again. This was only a temporary solution.

David showed him around the rest of the cabin, which didn't take long. It couldn't have been more than 1,000 square feet, although that was still bigger than Edgar's former apartment in NYC.

"I think I'm going to take a shower and go to bed," Edgar said as he stifled a yawn. He wasn't in the mood for bonding and figured cleaning up and then getting a good night's sleep would help improve his mood.

"Good idea, I'll probably do the same," David said, grabbing a towel from the hall closet that he threw to Edgar. "We should go shopping tomorrow to buy you some new clothes and whatever else you need. And I need groceries."

Edgar frowned as he thought about all his precious money in his bank account. He couldn't access it without the bank notifying the police. It would be too easy for them to track him down if he withdrew cash.

"What's wrong?" David asked.

"I was thinking about how much money I have gathering dust uselessly in my bank account."

David pursed his lips. "Right, I forgot about that. Well, I can help you out with stuff tomorrow, but you should probably find a job or figure out a way to earn money."

Edgar was about to agree with David when he realized something. "What do you do?"

David smirked. "I'm not sure I want to share that with you yet."

Edgar squinted his eyes in confusion. Now he was curious. "Hmm, okay. If I guess, will you tell me if I'm right?"

David paused, considering the idea. "Sure, why not? I highly doubt you'll be close, so I don't see the harm in it," he said, throwing his hands up in the air.

Edgar surveyed the cabin's main rooms again, looking for any clues as to what David's occupation was. There were several guns near the entrance to the cabin, but that didn't mean much. He lived in the mountains, so he probably liked to hunt. He hadn't noticed anything that would give away his profession, so he decided to blindly guess based on the little information he knew about David.

"Are you a writer?"

David laughed heartily and slapped his knee as if it was the funniest thing he had ever heard. "A writer? No, why would you think that?"

"I don't know. You live out here in the mountains by yourself. It seems like it would be a good place to inspire creativity." Edgar shrugged.

"Nope. What's your next guess?"

Edgar paused again. "Hmm, a park ranger?"

David laughed harder than before. "No, wrong again."

"Okay, I give up. I have no clue what you do."

David's eyes gleamed in the dim light of the cabin. Darkness had descended outside while they were talking and none of the lights in the main part of the cabin were very bright, so David's eyes seemed even darker. Edgar stared at the man who helped him escape from prison and saw something in him that he recognized, something that he had burning inside him too.

Chapter 29: Delia

After Delia tackled the blue-striped hoodie guy, he finally gave in and told them that his name was Blaine Fritz. Delia verified this by checking the driver's license in his wallet. After the hood of his hoodie fell off, she recognized him, but it was good that he was cooperating now. Carter was inexperienced in these types of situations, but he calmed down after Blaine was restrained. He probably felt less threatened with the kidnapper incapacitated. Only a matter of minutes had passed and surprisingly no one had walked by yet, but Delia knew they couldn't keep Blaine tied up on the side of a busy street in downtown Portland for long. A pedestrian or tourist was bound to walk by soon and either try to intervene or call the police, like any decent human would do if they saw someone tied up in public.

"Come on, grab him and help me carry him to our car," Delia said to Carter, deciding they needed to leave the area.

Blaine looked bewildered and terrified. He screamed and Carter immediately clamped his hand over Blaine's mouth to stop him from alerting anyone about what they were doing. A mom was walking by on the other side of the street with her toddler who was screaming that he wanted ice cream. Thankfully, the small boy's shrieks were loud as he pelted his mom's legs with his tiny fists and demanded a triple chocolate cone. The woman was preoccupied with trying to calm him, so she didn't notice the situation occurring across from her.

Delia and Carter managed to shove Blaine in the back seat of their rental car. Carter secured Blaine's hands so he couldn't unlatch the seatbelt to break free and they were off.

"Where are we going? Where are you taking me?" Blaine asked nervously, fumbling with the seatbelt as he unsuccessfully tried to unlatch it.

"You tell me," Delia said as she pulled the car smoothly out of the parking lot. "Where is Becca?"

Blaine laughed derisively. "I'm not telling you. You didn't find all the clues."

Delia slammed on the brakes and put the car back into park. She turned around in the driver's seat so she was looking straight at Blaine. "Well, at least you admitted you had something to do with her disappearance. I wasn't certain until now."

Blaine swore under his breath and Delia smiled. She and Carter were far closer to finding Becca than they had been earlier today. Following the clues had been the right move and following Blaine out of the coffee shop had been even smarter. This was going to work out.

"So, are you going to tell us where she is or will we have to resort to other methods?" Carter chimed in, cracking his knuckles threateningly.

"You aren't going to do shit," Blaine spat. "You're just her boy toy, flavor of the month, whatever… I bet you've never fired a gun."

"I am *not* her boy toy!" Carter said, temporarily forgetting their guise of being a couple.

Blaine smirked at Carter's reaction and looked at Delia. "Seems like you're not together then. So, who is he?" Blaine asked Delia. "I thought you worked alone."

Delia sighed. She didn't want to reveal any personal information. She only cared about finding Becca and making sure she was safe. She could deal with anything else that happened if she managed to rescue Becca.

"It's irrelevant who he is," Delia said.

Blaine became silent and struggled against the restraints.

"Anyways," Carter said, rolling his eyes and promptly attempting to change the subject.

"Where is Becca?" Delia jumped in.

"Fine, fine, I'll tell you," Blaine replied.

"Wait, you will?" Carter asked, as his eyes widened.

But Delia knew it wouldn't be that simple. He could easily lie about where he was keeping Becca. Or lead them into a trap. They didn't know if he was working with someone else. "What do you want?" she asked, gritting her teeth and trying to prepare herself for negotiation. There had to be something he was after. Otherwise, why had he kidnapped Becca and targeted her?

"Yes, I do want something in return," Blaine answered. "A small price to pay for saving your friend."

"Okay, what is it?" Delia asked.

"To be honest, my life has been really shitty since that day in the spring when I threatened you—"

"Wait a minute," Delia interrupted him. "You were waiting outside my apartment and tried to shoot me, but I disarmed you and stopped you from firing your gun. You were upset because of Clara's death. Is that why you took Becca? For revenge?"

Blaine smiled but didn't respond. He wouldn't make things easy for her. Why would he? He blamed Delia for the death of the woman he loved. He probably hated her.

Delia debated what she should do next. She could continue talking to Blaine and hope that he would give something away about wherever Becca was being kept. She could ask him outright again and hope he would tell her the location. Or she and Carter could rough him up a bit until Blaine gave them the location. She didn't want to resort to violence unless they exhausted their other options. She would continue calmly talking to him for now.

"Blaine, why did you take her? What do you hope to achieve from this?" Delia responded.

Blaine simply shook his head. "I can't tell you that."

"Why not?" Carter asked, putting down his gun in his lap. "Delia and I want to resolve this situation. We want to help you."

Blaine fidgeted in the seat more than he had been previously. Delia realized he loosened the ties around his wrists and was probably close to breaking free. If his hands weren't restrained, then he could unbuckle his seatbelt and leave the car.

"Carter, quick grab him!" Delia yelled as she unbuckled her own seatbelt and dove into the backseat of the car.

Blaine was halfway out the door by the time Delia was in the back of the car. She scrambled to grab his hoodie. The hood slipped through her fingers and Blaine triumphantly made a run for it. However, despite his appearance, he seemed to be out of shape. Carter easily caught up to him for the second time that day, and overpowered him. Carter punched Blaine in the nose for good measure.

"Okay, okay," Delia exclaimed as she stepped up to the two men, out of breath. "That's enough, Carter," she said with a warning look.

Blaine chuckled as blood dribbled down his nose. "Are you going to let her treat you like that, dude?"

Carter glared. "Of course, she's my boss, and besides that, I respect women."

"Right. So, Blaine, are you going to help us or not?" Delia asked for what felt like the dozenth time.

"Nope," Blaine said coldly, wiping a trickle of blood from his nose.

"Well, then I have no other choice but to involve the local police. If you won't cooperate with us, I bet the police will be very interested to know that you had a hand in Becca's kidnapping and have been holding her hostage for weeks," Delia said.

Blaine's face paled and he stopped struggling against Carter, whose hands were pinning his arms back. "Okay," he said quietly, finally seeming to lose his bravado.

Delia raised an eyebrow and stepped closer to Blaine. "I won't ask you again. This is your last chance. Where. Is. Becca?"

Chapter 30: Edgar

In the darkness, David stared at Edgar, leaving Edgar unnerved. He wondered again if he made the right choice in trusting him and what he would do if it wasn't safe to stay with him. He would sleep with his bedroom door locked, for one thing. But why was David staring at him like that? Edgar shivered as a sudden coldness seemed to permeate the cabin and David came closer to him.

"I have a secret, Edgar," David whispered, finally breaking the too-long silence that stretched between them for more than a few uncomfortable minutes.

"What is it?" Edgar whispered back, feeling chills crawl down his spine. He wasn't sure he wanted to know, but curiosity overpowered his fear, at least for the time being.

"I'm just like you," David answered, his dark eyes looking as black as the night outside.

Why were his eyes so dark all of a sudden? *He looks like a fucking demon in a horror movie.*

Sweat dripped down Edgar's back, despite the cold. "What do you mean, 'just like me'?"

"I think you already know," David said with a small smile, his white teeth gleaming in the dark. "Although, I've been better at getting away with it than you. I've never been caught," he said in a tone that suggested he was boasting.

"Shit," Edgar said as his mind churned through the mess to sort out what David had revealed.

"I'm tired though. I'm heading to bed. Goodnight. Don't let the bed bugs bite and all that," David said with a creepy smile.

David walked away to his bedroom and Edgar soon went to the spare bedroom. Edgar couldn't let himself think about what David was implying. If it was true, then why had he helped Edgar break out of prison? Edgar suspected he didn't want to team up with him. No, it was probably for a different reason. But what? He didn't know enough about David to make a reasonable guess, so he went to the bathroom to take a hot shower, then went to bed shortly after.

***

Edgar stood in the woods by himself, surrounded by nothing but trees as far as he could see in any direction. The mountains rose through the mist far off in front of him. The woods were full of blackness. He could only see the mountains from the light of the moon shining on them. Where was he? By the cabin? He looked around, but couldn't see the cabin anywhere. Had he been sleepwalking? He couldn't remember ever doing something like that, even as a kid, but maybe his subconscious mind was working in overdrive. After all, he had a lot to think about, not to mention, things to worry about.

He walked toward the mountains, deciding heading toward the light was his best bet at finding his way back to the cabin. He moved to check his pockets, but realized he didn't have any. He borrowed a pair of David's sweatpants and a T-shirt to sleep in, so that was what he was wearing. No pockets meant no phone. He walked for several minutes before he heard a strange noise. He stopped and looked around the woods again, squinting into the eerie blackness, trying to make out anything besides the ominous shape of trees. It was probably an animal. *I'm in Asheville*, he reminded himself. There were all sorts of animals in the mountains. He gulped as he thought about what types of animals could be with him in the woods at that second, prowling the forest near the mountains at night. Poisonous spiders and snakes. Coyotes. Bears.

The sound of a twig snapping came from behind him and he whipped around frantically.

"Is someone there?" Edgar called out, his voice shaky. He wiped his sweating palms on his pants.

There was no answer. Edgar turned back around to face the mountains and started walking again, only to hear what sounded like another twig or tree branch snapping.

"Hello?" Edgar yelled. "Hellooo? I promise I don't want to hurt you. I'm only trying to find my way back home," he said.

"That won't be necessary. You aren't going to make it back there," a deep male voice said in the direction of where Edgar heard the branch snap.

Was that David? Or someone else? Who would be out here in the woods so late at night?

Edgar still couldn't see anything, but his fear overwhelmed him, and he started sprinting through the woods as fast as he could. He hadn't noticed before, but he wasn't wearing any shoes. The rough, uneven forest floor was difficult to run over, especially while he could barely see and didn't know where he was headed. His bare feet became scuffed and cut open by branches, rocks, and God only knew what else as he ran through the woods. He heard the person coming after him and his heart pounded louder and louder in his chest, until he thought it would surely explode from his fear.

Suddenly, he was tackled to the ground by the person following him. The person loomed over him, and he could barely make out the mysterious figure's sinister smile and dark eyes by the pale light of the moon. It was David.

David pinned him to the ground and wrapped his hands around Edgar's neck, choking him. Edgar sputtered for air and struggled to fight David off. He thought he became stronger while exercising daily in prison, but clearly, he was wrong if David overpowered him so easily. Either that or David was unbelievably strong.

Edgar tried unsuccessfully to shove David's hands away from his throat, desperate to be able to breathe again. As he felt his oxygen supply diminishing to a dangerous level, his eyes closed, and all he saw was darkness. Then, there was nothing.

***

Edgar awoke from his nightmare with a desperate cry, which must have alerted David and woken him up because he raced into the room a moment later. Edgar sat up in bed, breathing heavily, clutching at his throat when David entered the spare bedroom.

"Are you okay?" David asked, as he swung open the bedroom door and flicked on the light switch.

Edgar squinted as the bright light illuminated the room and he realized it had all been a terrible dream. "Yeah, I'm fine. Just had a nightmare. It felt so real," he said shakily.

"Oh. Are you sure you're fine?"

"Yeah. I've been through a lot and after being in prison, my mind was bound to come up with crazy scenarios while I'm unconscious."

David stared at him stoically. "Wanna talk about it?"

"No, I think I want to go back to sleep. Thanks for checking on me."

David shrugged. "No problem. From the sound of your scream, I thought you were being murdered."

Edgar laughed nervously and pulled his hands away from his throat. "Night."

"Night," David replied as he turned off the light and shut the door.

Edgar laid back down in the bed, but didn't think he would be able to fall asleep again. He stared up at the ceiling, wondering if all dreams had a deeper meaning or if some dreams were simply a result of an overactive imagination. He didn't want to consider what his nightmare meant or if there was a possibility David was—That he was what exactly?

Edgar shook his head as if to clear it of all dark thoughts, but knew it was futile. Once an idea entered his mind, it was nearly impossible to rid himself of it. That was how he ended up in this mess in the first place. He couldn't afford to make any more mistakes. He needed to be more careful than before. He needed a safe place to rest and regroup before he figured out what to do with the rest of his life. He didn't want to live a miserable existence and now he certainly didn't intend to stay at the cabin. Besides, he doubted David wanted him to stay long. He wondered idly what David did for a living again, as he recalled their conversation from earlier in the night. Despite his anxious thoughts, his tiredness won and eventually he drifted off to sleep.

Chapter 31: Delia

Blaine finally caved and provided Delia directions to an abandoned factory near the edge of town. It was the only building on a forlorn looking street and took up most of the block. The lines for the parking spaces were so faded they were barely noticeable and weeds peeked out from cracks in the concrete. Delia surveyed the factory from the outside and surmised why Blaine chose this place to keep Becca hostage. Since it was abandoned, she presumed no one owned the building currently or there was no one who regularly checked on it. There weren't any other buildings or houses nearby, so no one would notice Blaine coming and going as he pleased, and supposedly no one witnessed him bring Becca inside.

Not wanting a repeat of what happened the first time they brought Blaine into their car, Carter sat beside him in the backseat to keep an eye on him while Delia drove, and the trip went smoothly this time.

When Delia stopped the car and parked in front of the factory, Carter pulled Blaine out of the car and shoved him toward the building.

"Lead the way," Carter implored.

Blaine huffed dramatically, but walked toward the back of the building. Delia assumed there was a back entrance he preferred to use for security purposes, but didn't want to take any chances.

"Is there an entrance in the back?" she inquired, pausing before advancing further.

"Yes, that's why I'm taking you this way," Blaine said sarcastically, shuffling along through the long grass that badly needed to be mowed.

Carter shared a look with Delia as if to say 'This guy though' and they continued toward the back of the factory. Blaine moved to take something from his pocket and Carter instinctively grabbed him to prevent him from pulling out a weapon.

"Hey! What are you doing?" Blaine asked angrily, spinning to look at Carter. He held a keyring in his hand.

"Oh. Sorry, I thought you were pulling out a weapon," Carter responded.

"You already took my gun from me!"

"Yeah, but you're clearly a criminal. Don't you sort usually have knives or some type of backup weapon on you?" Carter asked.

Delia stepped in between the two men to stop their bickering. "It's fine. It was smart of you to intervene, Carter, but he was only grabbing the key. Go ahead and unlock the building, Blaine," she said, nodding at him.

Blaine glared at Carter and unlocked the door, shoving the door open.

"Hold on," Delia said, holding her hand out to stop the two men from entering the building. "We aren't going inside until we have proof that you're the one who took Becca or evidence that she's here."

Blaine smiled slowly. "I was wondering when you would ask," he said, reaching into his pocket and pulling out his cellphone. He scrolled through his phone and stopped, turning the phone so Delia and Carter could see it.

Delia gasped and hurriedly covered her mouth at the horrific photo on the phone. It was Becca alright. And Delia couldn't tell from the photo if she was alive or dead.

She forced herself to lean in closer to Blaine's phone to make sure the photo hadn't been edited. "Can you show me a timestamp and the date you took the picture?"

Blaine narrowed his eyes at her, but scrolled back to his saved photos on his phone until the time and date of that particular photo popped up on the screen. "There. Do you believe me now?"

Delia nodded slowly. "Okay, let's go inside."

"Welcome to my lair," Blaine said as Delia and Carter hesitantly followed him inside the building.

Delia realized that even though Blaine showed her a picture of Becca, the factory could be booby-trapped. Blaine could also have a partner or multiple partners he was working with who waited inside the building to ambush them, so she remained cautious, holding her gun out, loaded and ready to shoot if they encountered trouble. Carter appeared to be staying careful as well, as he had his gun out and surveyed the small room as they entered.

Blaine was on the far side of the room, which appeared to lead to a hallway with a series of doors. "Come on," he said, impatiently motioning for them to follow him.

Delia and Carter proceeded cautiously after Blaine, each of them observing the hallway and watching the doors as they passed them to make sure no one else was in the building with them. Delia thought to herself again that she wished she and Carter had time to formulate some sort of plan, any plan, before they had ambushed Blaine and followed him. She hoped it hadn't ruined their chances of saving Becca. That was all she cared about at this point, besides making sure she and Carter made it out of this situation safely too.

The hallway was brightly lit. The polished concrete floor looked worn, as if it hadn't been maintained or taken care of in quite some time. The once white walls were more of a yellowish color and covered in imperfections and marks. Delia wondered idly when the building had last been inhabited and how long it had been since anyone besides Blaine stepped foot in the building. For all she knew, maybe he owned the building? She eyed his scuffed shoes, blue-striped hoodie that upon closer inspection looked like it had seen better days, and his faded jeans. She wondered what happened to him after the incident when he threatened her after Clara's death. He used to be one of the managing editors at *Women in Style*, the magazine Clara was an editor for, but if he had moved to Portland, kidnapped Becca, and was intent on exacting revenge on Delia, it didn't seem likely that he worked there anymore. Maybe the building had been foreclosed or he could have money saved that he used to purchase it?

Blaine abruptly stopped in front of her and Delia nearly walked into him.

"Whoa, sorry," she said.

Blaine gave her a side-eye and looked between Delia and Carter. "In case you didn't notice, the hallway ends here. There are a few more rooms to walk through and then we will be—"

"Where Becca is?" Delia asked hurriedly, feeling more anxious than before. Becca could be on the other side of the building and that filled her with joy and trepidation at the prospect of finding her friend because she was unsure what state Becca would be in, both mentally and physically. She also assumed that Becca was still alive because she didn't want to think about the alternative, but there was no guarantee. For all she knew, Blaine could have killed her after he took the last photo he showed her.

"Yes, yes, where your friend is. I want your word that you'll uphold your end of the bargain before I take you to her," Blaine responded irritably.

Delia nodded, but Carter eyed Blaine with obvious dislike.

"Are you sure about this, Delia?" Carter asked.

"Of course. Becca is the reason we came all the way to Portland. I'm not leaving without her," she answered fiercely.

"I know, but—" Carter glanced at Blaine, probably wishing he could have a private conversation with Delia. "I'm not sure if trusting him is the best move. It could be a trap. We don't know what's on the other side of that door."

Delia's heart pounded in her chest as she joined Carter in thinking about the possibilities that she tried to convince herself weren't plausible. But anything was possible. They didn't know much about Blaine, besides the fact that he thought Delia was responsible for Clara's death and at one point in time he worked as an editor. How did they know for sure that Becca was here? Delia felt stupid that she blindly followed a man who was nearly a stranger into what was potentially a dangerous situation, especially when it wasn't only her own life at stake, but the life of her partner who trusted her.

"No, you're right, Carter." She looked at Blaine. "Go into the room first and we'll follow you."

Chapter 32: Edgar

When Edgar awoke, sunlight already shone through the single window in his room. He scrambled out of bed, wondering what time it was, but then halted in his hurrying when he remembered he had no reason to hurry. No job, no friends, no life to worry about. He didn't have anywhere he needed to be. Most people would kill for such freedom. But was it really freedom if he couldn't go anywhere and had to remain anonymous?

He wandered out of the bedroom and into the bathroom to pee. He went to the sink to wash his hands and nearly jumped at the sight of the unfamiliar, exhausted looking man with clumsily cropped, light brown hair and dark brown eyes. He had forgotten about the changes to his hair and wasn't happy with his appearance. He vowed to make an appointment with a hair stylist as soon as possible to have a professional fix his hacked-off hair. Besides his hair, his face looked rough too. His skin was pale from being stuck inside most of the time he was in prison. He couldn't remember the last time he had been so unhappy with how he looked and thought back to the weeks after Jackson died. Edgar let himself go back then, stopped showering and taking care of himself, and overall gave up on putting any effort into looking presentable. But he looked even worse now.

Edgar exited the bathroom already in a sour mood for the day. He didn't see David in the small sitting room or kitchen, so he rummaged through the cupboards for breakfast. He found cereal, although the milk in the fridge was spoiled, so he ate the cereal dry. He ate sitting in one of the plush armchairs in the main living area. He noticed there wasn't a TV or any sort of electronics in the cabin. He assumed he wouldn't have Wi-Fi either then. Although it seemed a bit strange in the modern era, David must prefer to live off the grid.

After he finished his cereal, he walked around the cabin, checking out the main space for anything out of the ordinary. Edgar didn't find anything unusual and assumed David was still sleeping, so he decided to go for a walk through the woods.

Once he was outside, he saw that it appeared to be late morning already. The sun was out for the day, but not yet at its peak. Thankfully, the mountains near Asheville were a cooler part of the southeastern US, so although the sun shined, it wasn't unbearably hot. The air felt cool as Edgar walked into the front yard. Edgar didn't care much about the weather though. It was nice to be outside and not trapped in a tiny prison cell or confined to an enclosed yard. He was also thankful he slept restfully for the first time in months. He had forgotten about the nightmare that woke him in the middle of the night. And he was thankful that he could walk outside without being escorted by a pair of security guards, free of handcuffs, free to stay in the fresh air as long as he wanted. It was a wondrous feeling that he didn't think he would ever take for granted again.

Edgar thought about his escape from the prison and wondered what happened after he left or if James had gotten in trouble for letting him escape. He hoped not, but didn't care that much. He didn't become a serial killer for his overly compassionate and loving personality. He chuckled as he thought about all the people he killed. Except Jackson. Because that death would haunt him until the end of his days.

***

After his walk, Edgar lounged around on a lawn chair for several hours, enjoying the temperate weather and fresh mountain air. Maybe he would go on a hike later. He might as well fully immerse himself in the mountain life while he was here. When he considered going back inside the cabin to check on David, he came ambling up the driveway. Edgar didn't notice until David was closer to him, but his clothes, hands, and face were soaked in blood.

"Wh—what happened?" Edgar stuttered, quickly standing from the lawn chair.

David smiled, revealing blood on his teeth too. "I told you, Edgar. We're the same. Take a wild guess about what I was doing this morning," he said with a maniacal laugh.

Edgar's mind whirled. He didn't want to be living with a psychopath! He had escaped from a prison full of hundreds of pedophiles, rapists, and murderers. He told himself he was done dealing with those types of people.

"What did you—" Edgar started to ask.

David grinned even wider, making Edgar want to vomit from all the blood covering him. It was still fresh and dripped off of him in places.

David spread his arms wide as if showing off all his glory. "This is the real me, Edgar. There must have been something in our family's genes, since we both turned out like this."

"Is that possible? For killing to be hereditary?" Edgar wondered with fear before it fully sunk in what David said. "Wait a minute—"

"That's right. I'm your brother. I wanted to tell you sooner. I thought it would maybe help you trust me before your great escape from prison, but I also didn't want anyone to suspect me. I decided against telling you until we were safe. Now that we're here, I can tell you the truth."

Edgar felt dizzy and the world seemed to tilt. He sank back down into the lawn chair, trying to compose himself. "But my mom told me what happened to my brother when he was only an infant." He paused, reflecting on the little information his mom shared with him about his younger brother. "And she said his name was Eliot after T.S. Eliot, not David."

David laughed and said quietly, "I go by David now. My name was changed."

"But, how can this be possible? I thought you were *dead*. I thought I killed you," he stuttered.

"Well, whatever Mom told you was clearly a lie because here I am."

"Prove it," Edgar said, sitting back in the chair and crossing his arms over his chest.

"Right. I knew you wouldn't take my word for it. We're strangers. We never had the chance to grow up together, to get to know each other, to be brothers like we should have been allowed to. Here, I brought this picture Mom sent with me when I was a baby."

David pulled a worn photograph from his wallet and placed it on the table in front of Edgar. The photo showed an overweight woman with curled, vibrant red hair wearing a modest long-sleeve dress and holding a baby in her arms. She smiled broadly. There was a toddler at her feet, his hands folded in front of him, unsmiling, a serious expression on his face. Edgar recognized the younger version of himself and his mom, but was unsure about the baby his mom held in the photo. It could be anyone. His parents had tons of friends, especially when they were younger. It could have been any one of their friends' kids or a relative, or maybe a neighbor's baby.

"That doesn't prove anything," Edgar said, shaking his head and looking at the photo again. "Even if that is supposed to be you, you could have Photoshopped yourself into the picture. That doesn't mean you're my brother."

"Okay, I can see why you would think that. And I'm sure you've received a lot of crazy letters from people since your arrest. But I promise I'm not trying to trick you. I really am your brother."

"If you're my brother, then why did my mom lie about what happened to you? And more importantly, why didn't you try to contact me if you knew we were siblings? Why did you wait until I was in prison to come see me?" Edgar asked, staring down David with his haunting dark eyes.

"I'm not sure about our mom's reasoning for all the things she did. All I know is that she gave me up for adoption when I was an infant and left a letter with my adoptive family that they gave me when I turned 18."

Edgar absentmindedly brushed his hair behind his ears, momentarily forgetting he had chopped off his formerly long locks. "What did the letter say?"

"It said that she loved me and wished things were different, but my dad wasn't fit to be a father and didn't want another kid. She said I had an older brother named Edgar and that he was enough of a handful, so they couldn't handle raising another kid. She was sorry for the decision she made to give me up for adoption, but knew it was for the best, that it was for my benefit in the long run. But it wasn't," David said solemnly.

Edgar raised an eyebrow. "If you are my brother, then it was better that you were put up for adoption. You have no idea what I went through living with them."

"So, you believe me?"

"I'm not sure what to think right now. This is all a shock." Edgar paused. "Where did you grow up?"

"Near Minneapolis."

Edgar balked at the revelation. They grew up in the same city. They could have crossed paths over the years at school, on a playground, or anywhere in the city. It was ridiculous that he didn't know why they were separated as children. He cursed himself again for killing his mom while she still had so many secrets left to share with him. Then again, maybe some secrets were better left buried…

"I still can't believe my parents never told me about you. And we lived in the same city for all those years," Edgar said.

David sneered. "I doubt you would have wanted to meet me if you knew I existed sooner. You're only talking to me now because I came to visit you in prison and helped you escape, otherwise I bet you wouldn't have agreed to see me."

Edgar's eyes narrowed. "That's not true. I didn't know about your existence, so I'm not sure what I would have done. I still think I would have wanted to meet you."

"I doubt it. If I hadn't forced you to trust me and help you escape, then you wouldn't have wanted anything to do with me," David said angrily.

"I don't think that's a fair assumption, especially coming from you. You were the one who knew about me, yet you didn't contact me until recently. Besides, what did you mean when you said there must be something in our family's genes?"

"All sorts of traits are passed down from generation to generation. Why wouldn't killing be? It makes perfect sense. How else do you explain two brothers who were separated from a young age, grew up apart, and were raised by different parents, but both became murderers?"

Edgar thought about what David said and began to feel even more sick to his stomach. He wanted to leave. He needed to leave before David tried to hurt him. In a state of panic, he realized he had nowhere to go and no way to leave except on foot. He stared at David, wide-eyed with fear, wondering if this was the end.

"What's wrong, Edgar?" David asked, with a perplexed look on his face.

Edgar was silent. He didn't know what he was supposed to say after finding out his brother was a murderer. Besides, who had David killed in the middle of the mountains when there was no one around for miles? How had he found someone? Was it a lone hiker or a camper?

"Who did you kill?" he asked finally in a quiet voice.

David laughed harshly. "Is that what you're worried about? You think I'm going to get caught?"

Edgar paused, deciding that was the best way to go, although the thought hadn't entered his mind. "Yeah, you already helped me break out of prison. Killing someone near your cabin right after that doesn't seem very smart."

"Don't worry, they will have no way of knowing I killed that woman. She was hiking by herself on a trail a few miles away. I smashed her phone into pieces and then did the same to her."

He killed an innocent woman? Well, that explained all the blood. If David chopped a woman into pieces, no wonder there was blood splattered all over him. Edgar shuddered as he imagined the mess it left, his mind flashing back to the memory of chopping his dad into pieces with an ax. He wondered if David knew their dad was dead and how he would feel if he knew. That was different though. Edgar hadn't been responsible for that death. Their mom had been the one to kill him.

"Okay, as long as you were careful," Edgar said slowly, thinking about what he should do now that he knew the truth about David. "Anything else you need to share with me?"

David tilted his head to the side curiously. "Like what? Besides the fact that we're brothers and we're both murderers? What else do you need to know?"

"I don't know," Edgar responded, throwing his arms up into the air. The whole situation was ridiculous. "Are you keeping any other secrets from me?"

"I might have another secret or two," David said with a sly smile, advancing toward Edgar. "But as much as I would love to stay covered in this woman's blood, I need to go take a shower and clean up. I wouldn't want to leave any evidence behind. Unlike you, I don't plan on going to prison."

Edgar felt his anger simmering at David's comment, but decided to keep quiet as David entered the cabin. Edgar remained outside and sat back down in the lawn chair he had been inhabiting earlier. His world had been flipped upside down over and over again since he told his parents he was gay and was kicked out of their house. He thought back to that moment as the one that set the path for his life, instilling in him a distrust of people and fear of becoming close to anyone or loving anyone. He lived his entire life that way, with a fear of rejection. If he had told Jackson the truth, if he confessed his love to him, would Jackson have turned him away in disgust? Or would he have loved him back?

Edgar sat in the lawn chair, staring at the Great Smoky Mountains in the distance. He may not have known what he was supposed to do with his life, but maybe it wasn't too late to make amends and try to fix all the damage he caused, all the people he hurt. True, most of them were dead because he killed them, but he started making a list in his head of the people who were left, the ones who were still alive that he could reach out to. It was a small step toward redemption, but it was a step in the right direction.

Chapter 33: Delia

Blaine finally unlocked and swung open the last door, which presumably led to the room where Becca was being held. The large open space had the same worn polished concrete, but instead there were exposed wooden beams crisscrossing the ceiling that appeared to be rotting. There were pipes, an odd assortment of boxes and other things, perhaps left over from when the factory had been running. But most importantly, at the far end of the room, there was Becca, handcuffed to a horizontal metal pipe.

Delia cried out and hurriedly ran toward her. Carter grabbed her arm to try to stop her, but she shoved him off with so much force Carter tripped and nearly fell over. Delia raced to Becca and saw that her eyes were closed. She was unconscious. Becca still wore the outfit she had been abducted in, a thin-strapped, white tank top and plaid, cotton pajama pants. Her hair was disheveled and dirty and appeared stringy, as if it hadn't been washed in weeks, which was probably the case. Becca's face, arms, and legs were covered in some type of marks, scratches, or burns. Delia wasn't sure what the marks were from, but Becca was not in pristine condition. She anxiously checked her vitals. As a former police officer, she knew what to look for—the pulse rate and respiration rate. She had no way of checking other vital signs like body temperature or blood pressure, but she breathed a sigh of relief when she heard Becca's ragged breathing.

"Becca?" Delia gently called out, as she pulled Becca into her arms and held her. "Becca?"

Becca slowly blinked her eyes open and struggled to focus. "Please, not again" she whimpered; her voice raspy.

"Becca, it's me, Delia. I'm here to save you," Delia said, still holding onto Becca. "Please don't close your eyes. You need to stay conscious."

"Delia? No, you aren't here. I'm imagining—" Becca struggled to speak and her eyes rolled back in her head as she fell unconscious again.

Delia hypothesized if Becca had been tortured, she might have also been starved and dehydrated. Who knew the last time she had been given any food or water? She needed to bring Becca to a hospital as soon as possible, so they could give her fluids and make sure there wasn't any permanent damage. Despite her basic first aid training, Delia wasn't a doctor and didn't know much about medical issues or what the human body could withstand. She only knew enough to identify a dead body or someone close to death. And Becca was still the latter. For now.

Carter rushed over to them, waving his arms wildly. "Delia! It's the bookstore lady. She must be working with Blaine. We need to get

Becca out of here," he said, frantically pointing to the corner of the room where a familiar looking woman sat in a chair.

Delia had been so preoccupied with Becca that she hadn't noticed the woman sitting in the corner in a metal folding chair. Carter was right—she recognized her as the owner of the bookstore they found one of the clues in. But she was working with Blaine? Why? It didn't make sense.

Annie, the owner of the bookstore, stood from the metal chair and walked toward them, as if stalking toward prey. "Well, well, well… It's nice that you finally made it here. Although I'm a bit surprised it took you this long. Maybe you aren't as great of a detective as everyone thinks you are."

"I'm not a detective," Delia said, gritting her teeth and protectively holding onto Becca.

"Oh, cop, private investigator—whatever. They're all the same. All dirty with no sense of morals," the woman said with a wave of her hand. "Anyways, on to the reason you're here," she said, looking meaningfully at Blaine, who walked toward her.

At this point, Carter stood next to Delia and Becca with his gun held by his side. Delia didn't want to leave Becca, so she was grateful that Carter was beside her now. She was still unsure how Blaine and the bookstore owner knew each other. And she couldn't remember her name because they only had one brief interaction.

Blaine moved close to the bookstore owner and she rested her hand protectively on his shoulder. Delia's eyes narrowed at the gesture and she looked at Blaine. The bookstore owner was clearly much older than Blaine, so it would be strange if they were dating. Although, stranger things happened. Maybe she was a friend. Or a relative.

"Mom, I can take it from here," Blaine said, answering all of Delia's questions about their relationship.

Delia's mouth fell open in shock and the bookstore owner giggled at the expressions on Delia's and Carter's faces.

"Oh, honey, you ruined the surprise," Annie said, playfully nudging Blaine. "That's no fun."

Delia and Carter exchanged a look. Delia hoped they were on the same page. She didn't want to do anything rash and pleaded that Carter was thinking the same thing as her. She thought they could get out of the situation with Becca safe. If they couldn't bring Blaine and his mom into custody, then they could go to the police later and tell them what happened. To be honest, Delia didn't care what the local police ended up doing or even if Blaine was apprehended, if they made it out of the building alive with Becca.

"Why did you take Becca? And why are you two working together?" Carter asked Blaine and his mom, as he stepped closer to them.

Delia noticed Blaine's mom loosely held a gun in her right hand and hoped Carter noticed it also. She eyed the gun, feeling slightly better that Blaine didn't have any weapons on him. Unless he had weapons stashed away in the room or another part of the factory, which was plausible, especially if he spent a lot of time here.

Blaine's mom smiled. "Oh dear, Blaine didn't explain things to you? He was never very good at voicing his thoughts." She patted Blaine on the head, although he was easily half a foot taller than her and she had to step on her tippy toes to do so. She was surprisingly tall for a woman, at least several inches above the average height.

Blaine groaned. "Moooom," he complained, sounding reminiscent of a petulant child.

Blaine's mom chuckled. "Don't worry, Blaine honey, I'll take care of everything. Like I always do."

Blaine rolled his eyes and ducked away from his mom's hand patting his head. He shook his head as if to fix his hair, although it had been messy before his mom touched it. "I don't need your help."

"Of course you do. Every boy needs their mom."

Blaine huffed exasperatedly and moved a few steps away from his mom.

Delia sighed frustratedly. It wasn't going how she planned and she needed to get things back on track, so they could make their escape. "Okay, can one of you please explain what happened? Why did you take Becca?"

Blaine smiled gleefully, filling Delia with a sense of dread. "It will help if I start from the beginning. I used to work as the managing editor of a women's magazine called *Women in Style*. I started out as an intern and worked my way up over the years. I had a handful of employees I oversaw. Clara was one—"

"Sorry, but what does this have to do with Becca?" Carter interrupted.

Blaine glared at Carter and clenched his hands into fists at his sides, closing his fists tighter and tighter until his knuckles turned white. "Let me explain!"

Delia half-expected him to stomp his foot from the tone of his voice. She noted his change in personality from the instant he was near his mom. Clearly, it was not a healthy mother-son relationship. "Please continue," she said.

"Thank you, Delia," Blaine said stiffly, slightly unclenching his fists. He cleared his throat before he continued. "Clara started working for the magazine 3 years ago. At the time, she and Jackson were on a break. She was beautiful and clever and hilarious. Everything I had been searching for. All of a sudden, it made sense why it never worked out with any of my previous girlfriends. I became friends with her. I was in it for the long game, and besides, I was happy to be close to her. To talk to her and be there for her when Jackson was a dick. They inevitably got back together. She talked to me less and stopped confiding in me as much. But I hoped that she would realize Jackson wasn't right for her, and that I was—"

Now it was Blaine's mom's turn to interrupt her son's monologue. "You poor thing. It's such a shame what happened to her. Such a tragic event that could have been avoided. You would have had beautiful children," she said, shaking her head regrettably.

"Please. Don't. Interrupt. Me," Blaine said, spitting out each word with venom.

Blaine and his mom were both preoccupied with Blaine's monologue and weren't paying attention. Carter inched closer to Becca and leaned down to begin loosening the thick ropes tying her arms to the pipe.

Blaine's mom laughed breezily. "Such a temper, Blaine. You would think you weren't my son for how you treat me sometimes."

"Like my mom said, Clara's death was a tragedy that could have been avoided. Jackson's death was a shock to everyone. Clara didn't come in to work for a few weeks afterwards and when she did come back, she was a mess. She couldn't concentrate and I could tell she was falling apart. I helped her as much as I could. We started spending more time together, going out to dinner, meeting for coffee. She leaned on me for comfort. I thought—"

Delia was sitting on the floor, earnestly listening to Blaine's story and noticed his pause. She moved to block Carter, so Blaine and his mom wouldn't notice that he was working on freeing Becca. "You thought what?" she prompted.

"She was falling in love with me," Blaine said softly.

Delia and Carter were both quiet as they took in what Blaine said. Clearly, he was obsessed with Clara, even still after her death. *What is he after?* Delia wondered.

Blaine's pause for dramatic effect ended as he said, "Yes, she was falling in love with me. I know we would have been happy together. I could have given her everything. Maybe not the extravagant life she was used to with Jackson. But she would have been safe with me and I would have treated her like the queen that she was. You were supposed to protect her, Delia. Isn't that your sworn duty as a police officer? Why did you stop the security surveillance outside of her apartment? Why did you give up on the case when you suspected Edgar? Why didn't you do something? *Why didn't you stop him*?" he cried.

Delia's face darkened. As if she didn't regret what happened enough.

Carter hurriedly loosened the rope around Becca's wrists. Becca was thin, so the ropes were loose enough now that they could easily be slipped off. Delia suspected he was waiting for the right moment.

Blaine cleared his throat and seemed to partially regain his composure. "As the months passed, I became disinterested in my work. I no longer cared about the magazine, my friends, partying, or anything that I used to enjoy. It was as if all the light had been sucked out of my world. I followed the case after Clara's death, curious to see what would happen. You know that eventually I found out where you lived and confronted you outside your apartment. I was so angry at you for letting her die. I wanted whoever was responsible for Clara's death to be taken care of. You overpowered me that day and took my gun. You might have thought it was over and that you would never see or hear from me again, but it was far from over. I hatched a plan. My mom had been living in Portland for a while and owns a bookstore downtown, as you know. She's wanted me to move here for years, so I decided there was nothing left for me in New York and moved. I found this factory and purchased it. I had a lot of money saved from my job. I searched for any information about you that I could find. I soon realized that you didn't have many close friends, but you frequently posted about Becca on social media. I realized that was my way to get to you. At this point, you were involved in Edgar's arrest and he was in prison awaiting his trial, but it was too late. According to various news sources, Edgar committed several more murders before you finally found him and arrested him. All of those murders could have been avoided. You see, Delia," Blaine said, pushing his wavy blond hair from his eyes. "Becca was only a tool to lure you here. I knew you would come for her. And it's been fun the past few weeks; it really has. But it's all going to end now. You're the one I wanted. Becca and the kid can leave. But I'm going to kill you."

Delia didn't have time to react before Carter lunged forward and attacked Blaine.

"You're not doing anything," Carter said as he tackled Blaine to the ground.

Blaine's mom screamed shrilly and the gun she clutched inexplicably went off, the explosive noise echoing throughout the factory.

Chapter 34: Edgar

Edgar sat outside in the flimsy lawn chair until dusk descended, coating the mountains with the misty air that was now becoming familiar and welcome to him. He gazed at the view, enjoying the peace and beauty of nature. He didn't want to be around his brother. Besides, for all he knew, maybe his brother planned on killing him too. If that was the case, then he needed to be ready. Edgar knew that he had to kill David before he killed him. But he wanted answers from him before that happened. He wanted to know the truth—about David's supposed adoption, why their mom gave him up and lied to Edgar about David, formerly Eliot, dying, and why she kept them apart for their entire lives.

Edgar surmised he might not end up with all the answers he wanted. Their mom was dead, after all, so it was his fault if he never knew the truth about their family's twisted history. He regretted, not for the first time, that he killed his mom before he asked her everything he wanted to know. But at the time, all he thought about was her betrayal and his fear of being turned into the police. He never considered that he might have been able to convince his mom not to go to the police. Maybe they could have worked things out. But it was too late to regret the decisions of his past. What was done was done. All he could do was try to atone for his mistakes. And maybe get a few answers from David.

He decided to go back into the cabin and see what David was up to. Edgar walked into the main area of the cabin and found David sitting in one of the armchairs, staring into the gigantic stone fireplace, which was currently empty.

David turned to look at him when he entered the room and smiled creepily. "So, you finally decided to come back inside?"

Edgar seated himself gingerly in the other armchair next to the one David occupied. "Yeah, I thought it was time for us to talk."

David sneered and leaned back in the armchair, curling his legs up underneath him. "About what?"

"Our family. Our parents. Whatever you know about Mom and Dad and why they gave you away."

David's expression changed and his face suddenly looked pained. "I already told you most of what I know, Edgar. Besides, we both know Mom lied about what happened to me. I'm not sure why she wanted my existence to be kept a secret. All I know is they didn't want me."

Edgar's face softened. Sure, his parents hadn't been the best, not by a long shot, but at least they hadn't given him away as a baby. They raised Edgar and cared for him until he was an adult and came out as gay. That was the moment when his dad shunned him and his mom didn't do anything about it. So maybe Edgar had been abandoned by them too.

"I don't think they wanted me either, to be honest," Edgar responded after some hesitation. "They were fine as parents for a while, but they didn't know how to deal with me when I started killing animals. I see now that if they had gotten me help when I was young instead of ignoring me, my life might have turned out differently."

"Do you really believe that? You blame them for everything you've done—all the people you've killed?"

"No. I don't know." Edgar brought his hand up to his hair to stroke his hair like he usually did when he was anxious, momentarily forgetting again that his long, luscious locks were gone. He set his hand back in his lap.

"You aren't a victim of your environment or genetics or whatever. Sure, those things all shape you into the person you become, but ultimately, it's up to you what type of person you are. You can't blame our parents forever."

Edgar glared at David. "Don't you dare tell me not to blame them. You blame them too!"

Edgar paused thoughtfully while they both remained silent. "Do you know what happened to Dad?" he asked quietly.

David bit his bottom lip before nodding.

"Were you in contact with Mom then?" Edgar asked, his heart racing.

David fidgeted in the armchair. He avoided eye contact with Edgar and began to speak.

"When I turned 18, my adopted parents gave me a letter from Mom explaining everything. She left their home address in the letter in case I ever wanted to meet them. She said it was up to me if I wanted contact with them when I was an adult. So, I debated for a while if I wanted to meet them, then I went to their house one day when I was 20. They still lived in the same house all those years. Dad wasn't home that first visit, but Mom was there, so I met her. She seemed overjoyed to see me. I was unsure at first if I wanted a relationship with her or Dad, so I decided to take things slow. I went over there a few more times over the next few months. Dad was never home when I visited. She didn't want him to know she was seeing me. She said after they gave me up for adoption, he never brought me up again. And whenever she tried to talk to him about me, about her regrets and trying to find me, he told her to never mention my name again." David stopped talking, staring down at his lap, each of his hands clutching an arm of the chair.

"Yeah, that sounds like Dad, all right," Edgar said, shaking his head. "Some people aren't meant to be parents."

"No kidding."

"What happened after you started talking to Mom? Did you meet Dad?"

"I kept seeing Mom. I asked her if I would be able to see Dad. I wanted to talk to him and ask why he didn't want me. Why was he okay with keeping you, but he never wanted me?" David asked, the words catching in his throat as he became choked up with emotion.

"When he finally agreed to meet me, it was a letdown. I don't know what I imagined. Maybe I thought he would change his mind once he saw me and that we could begin to build a relationship, like I did with Mom. She tried her best to make up for all the years we missed together. But after he met me once, he said he had no interest in getting to know me. I didn't see him again for years."

Edgar pondered what David told him, doing the math in his head. His brother was about three years younger than him. If he met their mom when he was 19, that meant Edgar was 22 at the time. Edgar had been kicked out of his parents' house when he was 23, so he was still living at home when his parents supposedly met with David. Edgar's head spun as he tried to piece it all together and realized his parents lied to him and kept David from him, when he was right under his nose. Or was this an elaborate series of lies from David? The pieces didn't quite fit together and Edgar didn't know what to believe. He wasn't sure if it was better or worse to know the truth.

"If you're telling the truth, then I was still living with them when you contacted them," Edgar said, looking David straight in the eyes. "And they never told me any of this."

David stood from the armchair. "I have some whiskey in the cabinet. I don't know about you, but I could use some right now if we're going to continue this conversation."

"Sure," Edgar agreed as he grappled with the fact that not only had his parents abandoned him and cast him out of their home when they found out he was gay, but they also potentially kept this insane secret from him for years.

David returned to the sitting area several moments later with two glasses of whiskey. He handed one to Edgar, who accepted it with a nod of thanks and took a large gulp. David laughed at the expression on Edgar's face when he pressed his lips tightly together in disgust.

David sipped his own whiskey and smacked his lips appreciatively, relishing the taste and leaning back comfortably in the armchair. "So, after realizing our dear old Dad didn't want anything to do with me, I hatched a plan. I bided my time because I didn't want to get caught. I waited years to get my revenge on him for what he did…" he trailed off, drinking his whiskey and staring into the fireplace.

Edgar squinted at David, perplexed at this recent development. "When I visited Mom a few months ago, I found her dragging Dad's body down the basement steps. I helped her dissolve him in sulfuric acid, then I chopped him up into pieces and threw the rest of him into the lake in the woods behind their house," Edgar said calmly, as if talking about something mundane like the weather or what he ate for dinner.

David narrowed his eyes at Edgar and absentmindedly scratched his stubble on his chin. He paused before saying, "Okay, but I'm the one who killed Dad."

Chapter 35: Delia

Annie must not have been trained to use a gun or she didn't have good aim because the bullet traveled through the air, swiftly slicing through her son's shoulder as Carter tackled him to the ground. Delia gasped in shock and Carter jumped back from Blaine, a delayed reaction from trying to avoid the bullet.

Now it was Blaine's turn to scream. Annie rushed over to him, examining his shoulder and cooing at him that everything would be okay. The gunshot hadn't been fatal, but he certainly needed medical attention. Delia thought they could use the new situation to their advantage. If Blaine was injured, his mom seemed like the type who would go to the ends of the Earth for her son. She would probably want him examined by a doctor as soon as possible, which meant that 1. They would have to leave the factory. And 2. Delia and Carter could bring Becca to the hospital to have her examined too.

"We should go to the hospital now," Delia said, trying to maintain her composure. "He will be fine. The bullet grazed his shoulder, but the wound could become infected or he could suffer permanent nerve damage. The bullet might be lodged inside his shoulder still."

Annie sobbed over her son and practically shook him with her violent cries. It looked like she was injuring him further.

"I can't believe you shot me!" Blaine yelled, trying to shove Annie away from him.

"Oh, Blaine, I'm so sorry," Annie said.

Blaine clutched his shoulder, wincing as he attempted to see how bad the damage was. He gritted his teeth. "You're going to ruin everything. Give me the gun," he demanded.

Annie hesitated before handing her son the gun.

Blaine held the gun in his dominant hand. His injured shoulder was his non-dominant one. He pointed the gun at Delia. "I'll bleed out here before I go to the hospital. I don't care what happens to me as long as I kill you."

Delia inclined her head toward Carter, who finished taking the ropes off of Becca's wrists, and pulled her away from the pipe. At the same time, Delia lunged toward Blaine and slammed her gun against his head hard enough to knock him unconscious. Despite what he had done, she didn't want to kill him. All she wanted was to make sure he couldn't cause any more harm.

She bent to check his pulse as Annie yelped at the sight of her son's unconscious body. "He'll be fine," Delia said reassuringly. "Let's go to the hospital now."

Annie agreed and grabbed Blaine's uninjured arm, helping him stand from his hunched over position on the ground.

"We will meet you at the hospital. I'll drive my own car," Annie said to Delia, as she began to walk outside, half-dragging Blaine with her.

Delia moved to block Annie's path. "No, I'll drive the rental car and we'll all go to the hospital together," Delia retorted.

She didn't want to let Blaine and Annie out of her sight. If she did, who knew what they would do or where they would go? They could have an escape plan. Besides, she didn't know where they lived or how to find them again, other than the fact that Annie owned the bookstore downtown.

Annie sighed impatiently. "Oh, fine. Let's go now then. I don't want my son to have to wait any longer to have his arm looked at. He doesn't deserve to be in pain like this."

Delia restrained herself from lashing out as she thought about all the pain Blaine inflicted upon Becca over the past few weeks, and all the pain she would have liked to cause Blaine. Now she might not have a chance for that, but she was trying to do the right thing. If they went to the hospital, there would be questions and the local police would have to be involved. Delia wouldn't be able to exact her revenge on Blaine (or Annie, for that matter).

Carter and Delia lifted Becca and carried her out of the building, with Blaine and Annie trotting along slowly behind them. Once they were all crammed in the car, Delia drove to the hospital. Annie kept nagging Delia to drive faster, so her son didn't have to suffer longer. Delia tightly held onto the steering wheel and stayed silent for the entire drive, until Carter noticed her tension and placed a gentle hand on top of hers. She lightened her grip on the steering wheel and mumbled, "I'm fine," but Carter kept his hand there until Delia pulled the car into the parking lot at the hospital.

When Delia parked the car, the motley crew all tumbled out and headed into the hospital. Once they were inside, Annie immediately screamed for help, saying that her son was in desperate need of medical attention. Meanwhile, Delia and Carter exchanged a glance of loathing as they each helped carry Becca inside, who was in noticeably worse condition.

When they had a nurse's attention, she saw Becca's unconscious form first and rushed to grab a gurney. "Don't worry, we will help her," the nurse kindly assured Delia.

Delia watched the nurse grab a doctor walking by and they pushed the gurney down the hall to the first available room. Delia heaved a sigh—of relief, anxiety, or stress. She wasn't sure. Carter led her gently into the waiting room. Delia barely noticed that Blaine and Annie followed them into the waiting room. Apparently, no one had paid any attention to Blaine yet and he was still waiting to be seen by a doctor.

Blaine was awake now and complained for 20 minutes until a nurse came into the waiting room and called his name. Annie wanted to go with him, so she followed them into an examination room, leaving Delia and Carter alone in the waiting room. They sat in chairs next to each other. Delia had her face in her hands and couldn't keep herself together any longer.

"How are you holding up?" Carter asked.

Delia looked up at him and tried to smile. "I'm okay."

"That's what you said earlier, but I'm not sure if I believe you. How about I go find some snacks and maybe some tea?" Carter offered.

Delia nodded and sniffled. "That would be great, thank you."

Carter hurried off in search of a cafeteria or a vending machine. Delia sat by herself in the waiting room, wondering if her best friend was going to make it. She straightened in the uncomfortable chair, pulling for her inner strength and resolve that she developed when she worked as a police officer. If Becca didn't pull through, then she knew what her next move would be. She had tried to do things right. She hadn't wanted to kill anyone unless it was necessary. But if her sweet, innocent, best friend died because of this monster, then Delia would make sure Blaine paid with his life.

Chapter 36: Edgar

Edgar was still in shock that his brother admitted to killing their dad. He had assumed his dad died by his mom's hand and felt caught off guard by the surprising revelation. After all, several months ago, he didn't know about his brother's existence, and his mom dragging his dad's dead body down the basement steps didn't paint the picture of innocence. Besides, he knew their marriage was falling to pieces. It had been for years. Edgar never understood how his mom put up with his dad and how terribly he treated her, so it made sense to Edgar that she finally snapped and killed her husband. Now the real question was, did he believe David? Or was David lying to him to try to scare him or shock him?

"Why?" Edgar finally stammered, setting his whiskey down on the small table in between the two armchairs. "Why did you kill him?"

"He didn't want me. He gave me away and acted like I never existed. He didn't let our mom see me. My life could have been completely different if it wasn't for him," David said angrily.

"How did you do it?" Edgar asked. He had hated his dad for years, so he could almost understand why David did it.

"I poisoned a pie that I brought over one day when I visited. Mom wasn't a big fan of sweets and Dad was such a fat ass that I knew he would eat the whole pie." David paused and downed the rest of his whiskey in one large swallow and set his glass next to Edgar's. He leaned forward in his armchair eagerly, moving closer to Edgar. "Edgar, I know you understand. I told you before. We're the same. We both ended up gravitating toward death, despite growing up separately and being raised by different parents. What do you think that means?"

Edgar stared at David. "I don't know…" he said slowly.

David sighed heavily. "We're brothers, Edgar, not only by blood, but by our souls also. Don't you understand?"

"Sorry, I'm not sure what you're trying to tell me."

Exasperated, David leaned closer to Edgar and roughly slapped his hands down on either side of Edgar's armchair. "I think we were meant to team up together all along. Two brothers working together as serial killers? It makes perfect sense for us! Isn't it brilliant?" David grinned.

The color drained from Edgar's face and his heart raced. "I don't think that's a good idea."

David's excitement seemed to dissipate almost instantly. "What do you mean, Edgar? I'm not good enough to work with you? You prefer to work alone?"

"No, that's not it. I mean, I do prefer to work by myself, but that's not the problem." Edgar cleared his throat and took a sip of his whiskey, trying to give himself a bit of liquid courage to face the situation head-on, despite the uncomfortable burn of the whiskey. "I'm done with that lifestyle. I think this is my chance for a fresh start."

"A fresh start?" David laughed bitterly. "You've murdered countless people, including your best friend, your mom, and who knows who else. You're a serial killer. You can't erase your past."

"I'm not trying to erase any of my actions. I just want to—maybe try to atone for my mistakes." Edgar pulled a piece of notebook paper from his pocket.

"What is that?" David asked curiously, trying to look at what was written on the piece of paper.

"It's a list of people I need to apologize to and try to make amends with. All the people I've hurt who are still alive. If I can convince one of them to forgive me, then I think I can begin to move on and start my new life as a better person. I want to make up for what I did."

"You can't make up for it, Edgar. Those people you killed are all gone forever. They aren't coming back. No matter what you do now to make up for it, you can't bring them back, and that's the only thing that would make their loved ones feel better. Plus, I'm sure none of them want to talk to you. They all want you locked up in prison to rot for the rest of your life. They might want you dead. They would turn you in to the police in an instant if they saw you," David said logically.

Edgar bit his lip so hard that he could soon taste blood as he thought about what David said. "You're probably right. Then, what am I supposed to do? I feel so lost."

"Join me. If we work together, then no one can stop us. It will be a lot easier to overpower people, and take them down, and destroy all the evidence with two of us involved."

Edgar considered David's suggestion. It was a crazy proposal. Maybe a year ago or even a few months ago, he would have happily accepted and joined forces with his brother. At one point, he thought maybe Liam would be his partner in crime, but that hadn't ended well. Now all he could think about was the look on Jackson's face when he killed him. And how that death would always hurt the most.

Jackson appeared next to Edgar, standing beside his armchair, his face more decomposed and rotting than before. It had been a while since he saw him. "You're doing the right thing, Edgar. Don't give in to your killer instinct. Your brother won't look out for you like I did. He doesn't have your best interests at heart. He doesn't care about you and I guarantee no matter what he says, he'll turn on you."

Edgar nodded. Jackson was right. He remembered when Jessica visited him in prison and confronted him. If he wanted to take a small step in the right direction, then Edgar couldn't agree to his brother's evil plan. After all, he figured the first step toward being a good person was refraining from murdering anyone.

Edgar shook his head in disapproval. "Sorry, I can't do that. I don't want to be that person anymore. I don't want to be a killer anymore."

Chapter 37: Delia

Becca had extensive injuries. Her left arm was broken, she had several cracked ribs, bruises and marks all over her body, and she was severely dehydrated and malnourished. But the doctor reassured Delia that Becca was going to be okay. She was expected to make a full recovery. Delia had called Joel to tell him the good news. He had been ecstatic, and cried over the phone as she told him they found Becca. She didn't want to worry him with all the details, and of course Joel had immediately stated that he would fly to Portland and join them, so he could be with Becca. Delia told him to stay home and wait for them to return. She didn't want him to see Becca in such a state. It would be better if he waited. However, since Joel was a loving husband who had been worried out of his mind about Becca for weeks, he had ignored Delia's request to stay home, and was arriving on the next flight to Portland.

Carter proved to be a great source of comfort to Delia as she waited in the emergency room. She didn't know if she would have been as strong without him there and she was thankful for his steady presence.

Once she knew Becca was fine, Delia's mind began drifting again as they waited for hours in the emergency room. Edgar entered her mind like a sickness, a darkness that she could never fully eradicate. She knew what her next case with Carter was going to be. They had to prove Edgar was guilty of all the murders he had been accused of and make sure he could never kill again—

"Delia!" Carter exclaimed, shaking her by the shoulder and startling her out of her thoughts.

"What?" she asked, bewildered at the tone in his voice. "What is it now?"

"Look at the news," he said, pointing at one of the TVs in front of them.

Edgar's mugshot flashed across the screen. Beneath it, there was a scrolling banner that read: EDGAR PETERSON ESCAPED FROM MAXIMUM-SECURITY PRISON. HE IS A HIGHLY DANGEROUS SERIAL KILLER WANTED FOR MULTIPLE MURDERS. IF YOU SEE HIM, DO NOT APPROACH HIM. CALL LOCAL LAW ENFORCEMENT...

Delia gasped loudly and looked at Carter, whose face was rather white. "Oh my God..." was all she could say as she continued watching the news.

There wasn't much more information known about Edgar's escape, other than the fact that someone had hacked into the prison's security system, the power had gone out temporarily, and the backup generators had been disconnected. Supposedly, Edgar escaped when all the cells were unlocked. It had been chaos in the prison while the guards tried to ensure the inmates were under control and returned to their cells. No one had a clue where Edgar went or if someone helped him escape. Surely, he had an accomplice; otherwise, how would he have gotten away from the prison so quickly? He wouldn't have been able to accomplish a getaway on foot or by himself.

Carter was sitting up straight in his chair, staring at her, and probably wondering what she was going to do. "Delia..." he said carefully.

Delia shook her head, trying to convince herself to ignore this sudden turn of events. "I can't think about this right now. I need to focus on Becca and make sure we get her home safely."

"Okay, let me know if you change your mind and want to talk about it. I'm here for you," Carter said reassuringly.

"Thanks."

Delia sat back in her chair again after the news segment regarding Edgar's escape ended. She couldn't believe it. That slimy bastard somehow found his way out of a maximum-security prison. She shuddered as she contemplated someone helping him escape. Who would do such a terrible thing? Who would willingly allow a known serial killer to escape? It was sickening. But what she told Carter was the truth—she really did want to focus on Becca for the time being. She learned her lesson before. Family and friends come before risking your life to catch serial killers.

***

Becca ended up staying several more days in the Portland hospital. After Joel flew in, he refused to leave Becca's side. Delia and

Carter also spent quite a bit of time in the hospital waiting room, but at some point, Carter dragged Delia back into the outside world, telling her that they needed to experience all that Portland had to offer before they returned home. He reminded her that Joel was there for Becca and would make sure she was okay. Carter took her out to eat for seafood. They frequented nearly every coffee shop in town, and wandered the city each day until they were exhausted every night and nearly passed out when they returned to their separate hotel rooms. Delia wondered if that was Carter's plan, to keep her busy and distract her from thinking about anything else. If so, it was working. For the most part.

She still couldn't shake the feeling that she needed to go after Edgar and stop him once and for all, but couldn't bring herself to do anything about it. Besides, she wouldn't know where to start. No one knew where he was and there was already a nationwide manhunt for him going on. Someone else would find him. And why should it be her problem to deal with still? She did her part. She tried her very best. She had been the one to arrest him in Minneapolis in the spring. But a niggling little thought in the back of her mind told Delia it wasn't enough. It would never be enough until Edgar was dead.

After a few more days, Becca was due to be released from the hospital at last. Before their flight back to NYC, Delia and Carter decided to visit Blaine in the local jail, where he was being held until he went to trial. Currently, he was being held for kidnapping and aggravated battery.

When Delia saw Blaine in the visitor's room in the jail, she was filled with an almost overwhelming sense of rage. Carter gently placed a hand on her shoulder when he saw the expression on her face. Delia was so angry that Carter and Blaine could probably feel it in the air, emanating from every pore of her body. She knew it would be better if she stayed calm during what would probably be their last conversation with Blaine, but she couldn't rid herself of her rage over what he had done so thoughtlessly, without regard for the consequences, without regard for Becca's wellbeing. What would the lasting effects be on Becca and her mental health? How dare Blaine kidnap her best friend? How dare he harm her and think that he was going to get away with it?

Blaine sat in one of the chairs waiting for them at a small table, his handcuffed hands in front of him, and with a security guard standing on either side of him. He smiled when he saw them, which threw off Delia. "Hi, Delia. Carter," Blaine said brightly.

"Blaine," Carter said in acknowledgement.

Delia remained silent.

"So, what brings you two here to my lovely accommodations?" Blaine asked sarcastically. "I'm assuming this is going to be some type of interrogation."

Delia and Carter sat down in two of the empty chairs at the small, circular table.

Delia nodded curtly at Blaine. "You're right, Mr. Fritz. We have a few questions to ask you."

Blaine smirked knowingly, his lips curling up into a semblance of a smile. "I was waiting for you to come visit me. I knew you wouldn't be able to stay away. So, what do you want to know?"

"First of all, how did you kidnap Becca? I was taking my dog on a walk on the day she went missing. I'm assuming you broke into the house and took her while I was gone, but how did you break in? How did you convince her to come with you and bring her all the way to Portland?" Delia said in a rush, the words pouring out. She wasn't looking at her notepad and list of questions that needed answers. She was firing each question as it popped into her head. Seeing Blaine again had unmistakably rattled her.

"Ah, well the first question is an easy one. Yes, I kidnapped her when you were out of the house. I waited in my car a few blocks away. I watched the house for a few weeks so I knew yours and Becca's routines. I knew her husband, Joel, would be at work for the day, so he wouldn't be able to intervene either. I knew you always took your dog on a walk sometime in the morning, although the time slightly varied each day, so I had to be careful about how I timed my entry into the house, so that I wouldn't run into you. I wasn't sure if I would be able to overpower you, so I didn't want you introduced into the equation. You know how our first encounter went," he said with a light chuckle. "As far as the rest of it, I had a device that stopped the garage door from shutting when you clicked the button to shut it. Of course, this counted on you not double checking it after you started your walk, but you never did, so it wasn't an issue. For the next step, I entered the house because the door in the garage was unlocked. This was another chance I took, but I did have a lock-picking kit with me, although that would have taken more time for me to get inside, so I was glad I didn't have to use it. Once I was inside, I had to guess where Becca would be. I found her in her office and easily knocked her unconscious. From there, I left the note on her desk for you to find. Then, I drove my car close to the house and made sure you still weren't nearby. I carried Becca to my car and tied her up in the backseat and drove off to Portland."

Delia stared at Blaine, horrified at the details he revealed. It was all her fault. If she had locked the door inside the garage, if she had double checked the garage door was closed, if there were security cameras at the house—a dozen what ifs blew through her mind at all the things she perceived as careless mistakes she let slip by. If she came back to the house sooner, she easily could have stopped Blaine. After seeing how weak and whiny he was after being shot in the arm, she knew she could have stopped him if she had been there. She could have prevented it, if only she had been more careful.

"Okay," she said slowly. "So, why did you do it, Blaine? Why did you think that was a good idea?"

"I told you before. I did it all for Clara."

Delia shot a look at Carter to guess what he was thinking, but his face was impassive. He had a good poker face, which was helpful in this circumstance. Parts of Blaine's story still didn't make sense, but with a psychopath like Blaine, maybe his actions would never make sense to her.

"I didn't want to hurt Becca! I swear I'm a good person. She made me do it because she wouldn't listen to me. She kept begging me to bring her home and mentioning you and her husband, Joel. She said you two would come for her. It took you a while, but she was right," Blaine said.

Delia decided she would talk to Becca later and ask for her side of the story too, then she could compare both stories and find out what really happened.

"Blaine, I still don't understand why you left those clues for me to find. If you didn't think you could fight me adequately or overpower me, then what was your plan? Why did you want me to come for you and rescue Becca?" Delia asked as she glanced at her notes on her notepad.

"As soon as I found out you succeeded in arresting Edgar Peterson, I couldn't handle it. Losing Clara destroyed me. I knew Edgar was finally in prison where he deserved to be and that he would most likely receive a life sentence, but it wasn't enough," Blaine explained.

"Why wasn't it enough?" Carter questioned.

"Because you weren't being punished for what you did," Blaine snarled at Delia.

"Trust me, I've punished myself enough for that case already. I'm truly sorry that you lost Clara, but you kidnapped and harmed an innocent person. Becca didn't do anything wrong. How do you justify what you did?" Delia asked.

"You took down the great Edgar Peterson!" Blaine exploded. "I wanted to prove to myself that I was better than him, that you wouldn't be able to capture me. I never forgave you for the way you humiliated me that day outside your apartment. I honestly never thought you would find all the clues or that you would find Becca. I didn't think you were smart enough to solve the case."

"What about the creepy doll with the blue hair and buttons for eyes that you left with the note in Becca's office? Why did you leave that doll?" Delia asked, looking down at her notes again.

Blaine's lips puckered in frustration. "It's become a hobby of mine since I quit my job." He shrugged his shoulders. "I have a lot of free time and I like creating them, so I made a doll that looked like Becca. I thought it would add to the mystery of who took her."

Carter snorted and Delia shot him a look to silence him.

"Okay. The last thing I'm wondering is why was your mom, Annie, involved in all this?" Delia asked as she tapped her pen on her notebook.

"She was worried about me. She never minds her own business. I'm her only kid and she's always been a bit overprotective. She knew something was going on. One day, she followed me to the factory. She hid until I left, then went inside and searched the building. Of course she ended up finding Becca tied up and being held hostage, but instead of calling the police, she kept my secret. Despite her faults, she really is a good mom," Blaine said with a smile to rival the Joker's.

Chapter 38: Edgar

As soon as the words came out of his mouth, Edgar realized it had been a mistake. He should have lied. His brother instantly lunged for him and he jumped out of the armchair, away from David. His initial feelings toward his brother had been correct—David didn't want a brother or a partner in crime or whatever he claimed he wanted. No, he wanted to kill Edgar.

"What are you doing?" Edgar yelled, trying to fight off his brother with his fists raised in front of him.

David stopped coming at him for a moment and stared at him with his cold, black eyes. The same eyes Edgar had. The eyes of a killer. "Oh, Edgar, Edgar, Edgar… All I wanted was to know you. But none of this has gone how I thought it would. I thought you would be my *brother*, that we would bond, catch up on what we both went through, the traumas of our childhoods. I thought you would be the perfect partner in killing. We could have been great. There is no short supply of lone hikers and campers, or people who get lost in the mountains here. It's the perfect place to find easy prey, victims that will never be found, or their deaths are blamed on animals in the woods."

Edgar continued slowly backing away from his brother, hastily looking around the room for something he could use as a weapon. The fire poker by the fireplace was the best item he saw within reach, so he grabbed it.

David laughed harshly. "What are you planning on doing with that?" he asked.

"I don't want to hurt you. I only grabbed it as a precaution."

"You think I'm unstable, don't you? They all did too. That's why they tried to lock me away, but I ran away from home before they could put me in a psychiatric ward," David said.

"What? A psychiatric ward?" Edgar questioned, backing away until he bumped into the fireplace and he realized he was as far away from David as he could be in the room.

Edgar didn't want to hurt his brother. All he wanted was his rightly deserved freedom. Now he regretted it all and wished David never visited him in prison. Plus, what was he talking about when he mentioned a psychiatric ward? Was he mentally unstable? *I wonder what he did to make his parents want to send him away.*

"Yes, that's where my parents wanted to send me after I tried stabbing my adopted mom with a knife," David said, as if reading his thoughts. "My adopted dad was a big guy, so he stopped me before I could harm her. But after that, they never looked at me the same, and I know they didn't love me. I was better off on my own after I left the house I grew up in. They wanted to get rid of me," David said.

Edgar chewed on his lip anxiously and ran his hands through his short hair, wishing it was long again so he could stroke it and soothe his anxiety. "I'm sorry that happened to you. I really am. I was disowned by my parents too, so I understand how it feels to not be wanted by the people who are supposed to love you."

"Yeah, but they kept you, Edgar. You said they raised you and let you live at home until you were in your 20s. For my entire life, no one has wanted me, first my biological parents, then my adopted parents, now you…"

"I don't want to get rid of you!" Edgar lied. He needed to save himself and he would do anything to get the hell out of the cabin safely. "I was surprised at first to learn about your existence, but once I realized it was the truth, of course I wanted to know you. Sorry if I'm not an expert on being a good brother. I grew up without any siblings, so I don't know how I'm supposed to act," he fibbed.

David opened his mouth as if he was going to say something, but then stopped at Edgar's words. "Maybe I should have given you more of a chance," he muttered, "but it's too late now."

Despite how quietly he was speaking, Edgar heard the gist of what David said and hastily replied, "No, no, it's not too late! We can start over—"

"Edgar, didn't your parents teach you not to trust your estranged brother who you thought was dead?" David asked with an obnoxious laugh. He moved toward the rack of guns on the far wall, which were on the opposite side of the room from where Edgar stood by the fireplace.

Edgar knew he was fucked if he couldn't escape soon. He knew what was going to happen if he didn't make a move. By the time he charged toward his brother, David was already holding a gun in one hand. Edgar didn't know if it was loaded or not, but he surged forward and knocked it out of David's hand and brandished the fire poker in his face, hoping he appeared intimidating. He almost wanted to laugh at the situation. He was a serial killer, yet he had no clue how to fight. If he could grab the gun, however, he was great with guns. He loved using guns to kill.

The gun clattered to the floor. David tried to grab the fire poker from Edgar's hands. Edgar struggled to hold onto the fire poker as David attempted to wrestle it from him. He couldn't lose his weapon, otherwise he needed to get to the gun before David. He couldn't die now. Not when he had finally realized his mistakes. He still needed to talk to Jessica, at least one more time, and tell her he was truly sorry for what he did to Jackson. And while he was at it, he needed to talk to Jackson's parents too. They deserved an apology. He was surprised they hadn't come after him. This wasn't the way it was supposed to go. It wasn't part of his plan. It wasn't supposed to end this way.

Edgar and David each struggled to grab hold of the fire poker. Edgar finally loosened his grip, pretending his fingers were slipping and that he was about to let go. When David thought he had the upper hand, Edgar wrapped his entire right hand around the fire poker and shoved it into David's eye. David screamed in agony and tried to pull the fire poker out of his eye. He scrambled to pick up the gun that was laying on the floor by his feet. Edgar was preoccupied with the fact that he had stabbed David in the eye with a fire poker and didn't realize that David now had the gun in his hands. David pulled the trigger once, twice, and a third and final time. The first bullet missed Edgar because David's depth perception was off with a fire poker sticking out of one of his eyes, not to mention the immense amount of pain he was probably in. Blood poured down his face and blurred his vision. The second bullet hit Edgar on the right side of his chest. The third bullet went in Edgar's shoulder.

Edgar gasped for breath and clutched at his chest, as he saw the blood soaking his borrowed T-shirt from his brother. *That's going to leave a stain*, he thought sarcastically, trying not to focus his final thoughts on the fact that it was finally over. He would never find love again, even if he had wanted to. He would never become a Broadway star like he always dreamed. He would never be able to make things up to Jessica, Jackson's parents, or anyone else he felt he had hurt or wronged.

Jackson appeared beside him for the last time and stood over him, looking down on him with a sad smile. "Edgar," Jackson whispered in a voice full of emotion. "It wasn't supposed to end this way. You were going to try to atone for your mistakes. You finally realized what you did wrong, after all this time. It's not fair."

A tear slid down Jackson's rotting cheek. He bent down to kneel beside Edgar and held his hand while he thought about what Jackson was saying and tried to focus.

"Jackson…" was all he managed to choke out, as he tightly held onto Jackson's hand that was partly flesh and partly bone and began sobbing. Jackson was right. It wasn't fair that this was happening now. It should have been David who died, not him. He didn't deserve to die, but David did.

Edgar struggled to sit up, but Jackson pushed him back down gently.

"Shh, don't move," Jackson told him as he roughly stroked Edgar's cheek with a finger that had the bone exposed. "It's okay. I'm here."

This was it. The final curtain call. The long shadow of death had descended on the stage at last.

Chapter 39: Delia

Delia, Carter, Becca, and Joel flew home safely to NYC. Becca kept reassuring Delia that it wasn't her fault she was kidnapped and that she was fine now, but Delia continued to beat herself up over the situation. She kept thinking about how differently the events would have played out if she hadn't taken Lily on a walk that day or if she had checked that the garage was shut before walking away. All the things as a former police officer she should have been more careful about. Delia knew how scarred and traumatized kidnapped victims could be after the fact, even if they had a loving husband or family to come home to. It didn't change what happened to Becca and Delia would have to live with that guilt, just like she lived with the deaths of Jackson and Clara, like stones weighing her down, every day.

Delia was also trying to deal with the fact that she had blindly assumed Edgar was the one responsible for kidnapping Becca. If she had pursued other options sooner, then maybe she could have saved

Becca before she was harmed. She was thankful things hadn't been worse, and she would be sure not to make the same mistakes again. In her line of work, mistakes could cost lives, and she didn't want any other innocent lives to be lost.

On the afternoon they returned home from Portland, Delia received an email from a woman who was battling for custody of her kids. She wanted dirt on her ex-husband to prove that she was the better parent to raise their kids. She wanted to hire *Wilson Investigative Services*. She didn't have a lot of money and it wouldn't be a high-paying case, but Delia felt sorry for the woman. She took the case because she knew this was the sort of case she should be working on. She could help this woman build a better life for herself and her kids. Delia was hopeful that more cases would start coming in soon.

***

A few days later, Delia sat at her desk in her bedroom. She was supposed to be meeting with Carter later to discuss their next case. Although cases had been slowly trickling in, they needed a case that would earn them a substantial amount of money, especially if Delia wanted to hire Carter permanently after his probationary period was over. *Wilson Investigative Services* currently wasn't earning enough profit to pay herself, let alone an employee, or necessary business and living expenses. The only way she made it this long was because she had managed to obtain a small business loan from the bank, which was paying all the necessary business expenses for now. But the money would run out eventually. Something had to change if Delia wanted to continue working for herself and not return to a job where she would most likely be miserable.

A knock came on her bedroom door and she turned in her chair to face the door.

"Come in," she called, assuming it was Becca.

Surprisingly, Joel was at her door. "Is it okay if I come in for a minute?" he asked, fidgeting with the collar of his short-sleeved polo shirt.

"Sure."

Joel shut the door.

"I know I've said thank you already, but seriously, Delia—"

"You've only thanked me about a hundred times. Joel, I know you appreciate it. Trust me, I'm glad she's home too."

Joel sighed and stopped fidgeting with his collar finally. "Okay, but that's not the only thing I wanted to say to you…"

"Well, don't keep me in suspense then."

"Do you think Becca is going to be okay?" Joel blurted out.

"What do you mean?" Delia asked nervously. Physically? Sure, she would heal. Mentally and emotionally? She would probably have scars for the rest of her life.

"I mean that she doesn't seem like herself since she got home." Joel hung his head and paced back and forth in the bedroom.

"Joel, it's only been a few days. And Blaine held her captive for weeks. That's not something you can just—"

"I know. That's why I wanted to talk to you. I'm trying to be there for her, to help her through the healing process from all that she endured. But she's not opening up to me like she used to. She doesn't want to talk about it. And I don't know how to help. I'm at a loss…"

Delia patted Joel on the shoulder. "You're a good husband, Joel. Becca is lucky to have you in her life. She knows you're there for her.

She needs time though. I'm sure she will talk to you about it eventually. Be patient with her."

"Right. I suppose I'll continue doing what I've been doing. Do you think a date would cheer her up? Maybe at a nice restaurant?"

"I don't know if she's ready for that yet, but you could ask her and see if she's feeling up to it. Her face is plastered all over the news right now, so she might not want to go out in public in case people recognize her."

"You're right, it was a stupid idea. I'll think of something else," Joel said.

Delia laughed lightly. "It wasn't stupid. But I'm sure you'll come up with something."

A small smile emerged on Joel's face. "Thanks." He turned to leave the bedroom and exhaled loudly, pausing with his hand on the doorknob.

"Anything else you wanted to talk about?" Delia asked, raising an eyebrow.

"For the first time in a long time, I feel like there's hope. Hope for our future and our lives together, mine and Becca's, I mean."

"I knew what you meant," Delia said with a chuckle. "I'm glad though. I've always thought about how lucky you two were that you found each other."

Joel scoffed. "Luck doesn't have anything to do with it. We were teenagers when we fell in love, but we worked to build our relationship into a strong one, and that work took years. Anything worth having takes time and effort." Joel paused and stroked his chin. "What about you and Carter? You two seem to get along," he said with a mischievous smile.

Delia's face flushed and she could tell it was turning red. "Oh God, no," she stuttered, trying to rid herself of her obvious embarrassment at Joel's question. "He has a girlfriend. Besides, he works for me. And he's much too young."

Joel rolled his eyes. "Sounds like you're making up excuses. But what do I know?"

***

Later that day, Delia was in one of the meeting rooms in the library, waiting for Carter to arrive. He was one of the most punctual people to exist, so she knew he would probably arrive early. They were going to discuss how to find Edgar. Delia had tried focusing on other things. For example, her best friend being kidnapped and held captive by someone she pissed off had been a distraction for the last few weeks. But now that Becca was home, Delia's mind gravitated back to Edgar. She started watching the news again and was on the lookout for any information or updates regarding Edgar's whereabouts. She vaguely wondered if she should travel to Minneapolis and talk to the head of the prison and the security guards who worked there. There had been at least one prison guard stationed outside of Edgar's cell at all times, so how did he escape? Going to the maximum-security prison might be the only lead she had for now. Maybe she could call them this time instead. She couldn't afford to keep frivolously traveling for a case that wasn't going to bring in profit.

Carter arrived and joined her at the table in the private meeting room, where they worked for a few hours on the child custody case that Delia had recently received. After their initial research on their new case, she told him what she had been thinking about Edgar. She waited patiently for his response, thinking she might have to convince him that it was the right move. After all, going after a notorious serial killer would be dangerous. But when Delia finished speaking, Carter immediately agreed.

"I think your idea sounds good. Since his parents are dead and he doesn't have any other known family or friends, the prison is the best place to start."

"Okay, then I'll try calling the prison tomorrow. If we get a lead, then we can figure out where to start looking for Edgar," Delia said.

"Yup, and I think we should leave as soon as we know where to look. It's already been a week since he escaped from the prison. He could be anywhere by now."

"You're right." Delia swallowed louder than she intended, her mouth suddenly dry, not wanting to scare him, but also striving for honesty with her partner. "You do understand that this is going to be dangerous. So, there's a chance we won't come home."

Carter stared at his hands and the pen and notebook in his lap before looking up at her. "Okay, I know you're trying to make sure I'm prepared, but don't worry. I know what I'm getting into and that there are risks. I didn't choose this career because I thought it would be safe and easy," he said with a grin.

Delia smiled back. "As long as you understand."

"Yup. Is it okay if I spend tonight with my girlfriend then, since there's a chance we could be leaving in the next few days?"

"Of course. I'll call you and let you know what I find out."

"Sounds good," he said, flashing a smile at Delia as he left.

Delia planned to call the prison tomorrow. She would request to talk to the prison warden or any guards that might have been watching Edgar, and hopefully obtain some helpful information, then plan their next move. In the meantime, she needed to talk to Becca and check in to make sure she was okay.

Delia left the library shortly after Carter. She arrived at home 20 minutes later. After hanging her bag in the closet in her bedroom, she walked down the hallway to Becca and Joel's bedroom and knocked on the door a few times.

"Come in," Becca called, and Delia opened the door.

Becca was lying in bed, propped up by three pillows, with a quilted comforter spread over her. Unlike her usual look, she wasn't wearing any makeup. She paused the TV, which appeared to be playing "American Horror Story: Asylum."

"Where's Joel?" Delia asked as soon as she realized he wasn't in the bedroom with Becca.

"He went to pick up dinner. He's trying so hard to make everything go back to normal," Becca said with a small sigh.

"He only wants the best for you," Delia said, walking further into the bedroom and plopping herself down on the bed next to Becca. "You know he would do anything for you."

"I know. Things can't go back to the way they used to be though. I'm not the same."

"I understand. You need time to rest and heal your mind and body."

"Yeah, but Joel thinks now that I'm home I should start writing again to take my mind off of what happened. But I don't feel like writing."

"I'm sure Joel doesn't want you to push yourself. He wants you to be happy and he knows that writing has always been your passion."

Becca shook her head vigorously. "He wants me to be the same as I was before. But I'm not. Everything feels different. I was so scared. And alone. I thought I was going to die and I couldn't even be brave while I was being held there. I begged him to let me go over and over. I couldn't handle it."

Delia's eyes brimmed with tears and she hurriedly wiped them away. She needed to reassure Becca, not make her feel worse by falling apart in front of her. She rested her hand on top of Becca's. "You're safe now, Becca, and nothing like that is going to happen to you again."

Becca squeezed Delia's hand. "I appreciate the sentiment, but you can't guarantee that." A few tears slid out of Becca's eyes and she brushed them off her face. "Was there something you wanted to talk about or did you come in here to check on me? Because I would like to return to my show," Becca said, pointing at the screen where the AHS opening was frozen on a gruesome image.

"I wanted to let you know that Carter and I will be leaving for a case this week. Maybe as soon as tomorrow. I have to call the prison tomorrow to see what they know about his escape. We might be gone for a while if we can't get the information we're looking for."

Becca groaned. "Oh, come on, Delia. This isn't about Edgar again, is it?"

Delia smiled sheepishly. "Yes, it's regarding Edgar. I need to end this. I need to make sure he can't hurt anyone else."

"Why is that your responsibility? You already arrested him once. It's not your fault he escaped from prison. You and Joel keep telling me to move on from what happened, but you haven't moved on from what happened to you. It's going to keep tearing you up inside unless you find a way to let it go and move on with your life."

Delia frowned, not wanting to admit that Becca was right. Her best friend always seemed to know what she was thinking. It was a rare connection that she had never felt with anyone else. Delia hugged Becca and Becca responded by hitting her with one of her pillows.

"You're going to ignore what I said and try to find Edgar, aren't you?" Becca said knowingly.

Delia stood from the bed. "I have no idea what you're talking about," she said as she stood from the bed.

"Please don't do anything stupid," Becca pleaded, her eyes shining with tears. "I couldn't bear it if something happened to you."

"Don't worry, I'm not going by myself. I'll have Carter with me. Besides, I'm a badass. I'll be fine," Delia responded with an airy laugh, leaving the bedroom and shutting the door before Becca could protest any further.

Chapter 40: Delia

Early the next morning, Delia called the Harriet Heights Maximum Security Prison. The prison warden remembered her since she was involved in Edgar's arrest and had visited him several times. Although she was no longer a police officer, since her call was related to Edgar Peterson's escape, the prison warden was soon on the phone with her. Delia could only assume how unhappy he was about Edgar being the first person to ever break out of the prison. Besides the fact that a serial killer was on the run, it also didn't help the prison uphold its reputation.

There was silence on the phone as Delia waited several moments for the prison warden to pass the phone off to James, one of the prison's guards who was regularly in charge of Edgar's security.

"Hello, Delia? I'm James." A man's voice sounded from the phone.

"Hi, James. Thanks for agreeing to talk to me. I'm sure you're busy, so I promise to not take up too much of your time."

James cleared his throat. "I understand from what the warden told me that you called to speak about Edgar Peterson, one of our inmates."

"Yes, I have a vested interest in his whereabouts," Delia said. "I'm a private investigator and was involved in his arrest in April."

James paused curiously. "Huh, okay. So, what kinds of questions do you have for me?"

"First of all, you were one of the prison guards who regularly watched his cell. Correct?" she asked.

"Yeah, but there are dozens of other guards who work here. It's a large prison, the only maximum-security prison in the state. I wasn't the only person who interacted with Edgar on a regular basis," James replied defensively.

"The warden mentioned that you and Edgar often seemed to be chatting. He thought Edgar might have trusted you," Delia said.

"Well, we were friendly, sure, but I try to be nice to all the guys here. Some of them have had pretty rough lives and not all of them deserve to be locked away. Some of them are innocent, but were at the wrong place at the wrong time or forced to take the fall for someone else," James explained.

"Do you think Edgar is one of those people?" Delia asked.

"An innocent person? Maybe," James said thoughtfully. "I can't say for certain, but he was always friendly to me."

"Did you see him the day he escaped?"

"Yes."

"Were you the one watching his cell when he escaped?"

"No, of course not! I would never willingly let an inmate escape," James protested.

"Not even someone you thought was innocent? Someone you were friends with, perhaps?"

"Look, I understand where you're going with this, so I'm going to tell you what happened. On the day Edgar escaped, someone hacked the prison's security system. Then, the power went out. It takes a few minutes for the back-up generators to power on because they're old and should probably be replaced. All the cells were unlocked during that time and none of the alarms were working either. So, that's how Edgar got out. But I don't know how he got away so fast or where he went," James said in a rush.

Delia pondered the facts she knew so far, and reconsidered the questions she wanted answered. "Did Edgar have any visitors besides me since he was brought to the prison?"

"His lawyer. I don't think anyone else ever came," James said, shrugging his shoulders.

"Hmm, okay. One of my theories is that Edgar was working with someone else. That he had a connection outside of the prison who helped him escape," Delia explained.

There was a moment of silence. "Wait, I do remember another visitor. His name was David. He said he was Edgar's friend."

"What?" Delia yelled; her voice suddenly much too loud in her shock.

"Yeah, he said he was Edgar's old friend from when they were kids. He started visiting him a few weeks ago and came here a few times. He said he hadn't seen Edgar in years and wanted to get to know him again and bond with him. He must have seen the news about Edgar's arrest and found out he was here," James said.

"Do you know where he lives? Is it somewhere in Minnesota too?"

"No, I remember he mentioned making the long drive here, which is why he couldn't visit more than once a week. I'm not sure where he lived, but I could ask the warden for the information and send it to you later," James said.

"That would be extremely helpful. Thank you," Delia said.

"Anything else?" James asked.

"No, I think that's it for now. I'll call the warden if I have any further questions. You've been a great help," she told James and then hung up the phone.

I think we might be able to catch him. And this time, I'm going to make damn sure he never kills again, she thought to herself.

***

Delia hoped that soon she would hear from the prison warden and have a lead on where Edgar's friend lived. Would he really be so dumb that he would have used his real address and contact information when he visited the prison? And why hadn't anyone in the prison already followed this lead? Didn't they suspect David of helping Edgar?

For the hundredth time, Delia contemplated what made Edgar turn out the way he did. It must have something to do with his past, perhaps the way his parents raised him or a traumatic event that happened to him when he was younger. She knew childhood trauma could bring out the worst in people and leave a lifelong impression. She supposed the explanation for the way he was didn't matter much if she caught him, but she couldn't stop herself from being curious.

The mind of a serial killer was intriguing; how did someone become so twisted and evil that they could kill not just one or two, but at least three people? Delia thought it was a topic a lot of cops and law enforcement officers wondered about because they dealt with all sorts of criminals and sometimes the dregs of society.

At 11:00 p.m., Delia was still awake. She kept the TV on, but she wasn't paying attention to what was on the screen. Instead, she had her notebook and piles of notes spread out on her bed so she could look over everything at once. She felt the same as she did back in April, when she was so close to finding Edgar, the anticipation and anxiety building, but she still needed *one more clue* before locating him. She idly wondered if Edgar would be found or if he would ever stay in prison. What if he really vanished this time? He was a master at making himself disappear. He already disappeared once before, so he must have a better idea of how to remain undetected. The difference was that this time he somehow managed to escape from a maximum-security prison that no one had ever been able to escape from, adding another item to his list of crimes. Even if he wasn't found, Edgar Peterson would be a household name for years to come.

Delia finally managed to fall asleep. She was exhausted and drifted off while she was still sitting up and leaning against the headboard, with her notes all over the bed and the TV still on. She woke up a few hours later, stacked her notes in a pile that she placed on the dresser, and turned off the TV. She climbed under the covers and pulled them up to her chin, sighing sleepily as she tried to will herself back to sleep.

The next morning, Delia awoke groggily to her cellphone buzzing on the nightstand beside the bed.

"Hello?" she answered to an unknown phone number.

"Delia Wilson? This is Michael, the prison warden at the Harriet Heights Maximum Security Prison."

"Oh, hi, Michael. How are you?"

"Good. I'm calling to provide the address of David Chester, the visitor you were asking about yesterday. I'm not sure why you want it though. We have no reason to believe that Edgar was working with David. He was also visited by a woman named Jessica Birkman, so for all we know, she was involved in the escape. Most likely, Edgar escaped when the power went out and is somewhere near the prison still. There are officers and a search team scouring the area. He couldn't have gotten very far on foot. Besides, I already handed over the names and contact information and all other relevant information about Edgar's escape to local law enforcement."

"I understand, but I know Edgar. I think this is worth investigating."

"They're interviewing the rest of his visitors and searching here before they involve the North Carolina police force too. I imagine they tried contacting David already, but if they haven't yet, then they'll be knocking down his door before too long."

Delia bit her tongue and refrained from saying they were making a stupid decision by not pursuing David immediately if they had his address. It didn't matter. She would find Edgar herself.

"What's the address?"

Michael provided David's address and the conversation ended. Delia quickly Google searched the location. It was a cabin in western North Carolina near Asheville. Not anywhere near New York, where she currently was. She sighed in frustration. Of course things couldn't be simple and David didn't live close by. She decided to purchase one-way flights to Asheville for herself and Carter. She could buy the return flights later, after they knew when they would be heading home. She also needed to notify Carter that they would be leaving soon.

Delia threw on an outfit and packed the items she would need for their trip into her small carry-on. She decided to call Carter to give him as much notice as possible. She wasn't sure if he was an early riser, but she was surprised by how quickly he answered his phone.

"Oh! I wasn't sure if you would be awake yet," she said when he answered.

"Yeah, barely slept. Well, what's up?" Carter replied, sounding annoyed.

Delia decided to ignore his tone. He said he didn't sleep well, so maybe that was it. That didn't mean anything else was wrong. "I heard from Michael, the prison warden, and he gave me Edgar's friend David's address. Besides me and his lawyer, the only other people who visited Edgar in prison are Jackson's sister, Jessica, and his friend, David. I highly doubt Jackson's sister would help Edgar escape, so it had to be David."

Carter heaved a sigh. "Okay. So, where are we off to now?"

"Asheville, North Carolina. Our flight leaves in the afternoon. Pack your stuff and I'll meet you at the airport in a few hours."

"Sounds good."

Delia wondered again if Carter was just tired or if something else was bothering him. Whatever it was, something seemed off. But she couldn't worry about that now. They were so close to finding Edgar and she was determined that this time would be the last time she had to deal with him. She hadn't wanted to think about it before, but she would do what was necessary, even if it meant she had to kill Edgar.

Chapter 41: Delia

Delia and Carter arrived in Asheville, North Carolina in the late afternoon after what seemed like an extremely long day. Going from one flight to another and traveling all day was exhausting. Once they picked up their rental car, Delia drove more cautiously than usual through the mountains. The Blue Ridge Parkway was known for being one of the most scenic drives in the United States, but Delia couldn't appreciate the beauty because the lack of guard rails in the mountains made her paranoid about driving off the road and down a cliff. After about 20 minutes, Carter directed her to pull off down a gravel road. There weren't any other buildings or houses around. They hadn't seen other people for miles either. All they saw were trees, wildlife, and the Great Smoky Mountains covered in a haze that made them barely visible from their current vantage point.

Delia pulled the car into the driveway of the cabin that David had listed as his address and parked the car.

"Okay, we need to act fast because we don't know if Edgar is working with David or what is going on. They might not be home, but they probably have the place trapped for instances like this. They most likely anticipated the police would come for Edgar. He might have assumed I would be after him. And wherever they are, they're probably armed and dangerous," Delia explained, grabbing her gun from the backseat.

"Well, there is a car in the driveway, so maybe at least one of them is home?" Carter said, looking around and pulling out his own gun from his bag.

They exited the car together, slowly surveying their surroundings and checking out the outside of the small log cabin. They didn't notice anything that appeared to be suspicious or dangerous, so Delia proceeded to open the front door, which was unlocked and instantly sent a red flag. The only possibilities that made sense were 1. David lived in the mountains with no close neighbors, so he felt safe enough to leave his cabin unlocked. Or 2. David and Edgar were waiting inside, ready for an ambush, and left the cabin unlocked on purpose so anyone could easily walk inside without disturbing them.

As soon as they entered the cabin, Delia and Carter both started gagging and hastily covered their mouths with their hands from the stench that permeated the air. As they entered the main room of the cabin, they realized where the smell emanated from. Edgar's decomposing body was arranged in a seated position in one of the oversized, plush armchairs in the sitting room. It was obvious as they inched closer that Edgar hadn't just died. His body looked as if it had been there for a few days.

Delia gasped at the sight of her former nemesis rotting in front of her. "Oh my God…"

"Do you think David killed him?" Carter asked, looking around the cabin nervously, most likely wondering where David was and if he was hiding somewhere and waiting for his chance to jump out, catch them off guard, and kill them.

"I don't know, but we need to report this to the local police and the Harriet Heights Maximum Security Prison, so they know he's dead and cease their manhunt. I can't believe it…"

Carter looked at her imploringly. "Are you disappointed?" he asked.

"About what?"

"That you weren't the one to—you know."

"As much as I hoped that he would spend the rest of his life in prison, so the rest of humanity would be safe from him, I didn't want to kill him. I only wanted justice," Delia said.

It was the truth. She was relieved that she hadn't been the one to kill Edgar. Her reputation wasn't tainted and her conscience was clear. Edgar was gone and he couldn't harm anyone else. Now if only they could find his friend…

"Ahhhh!" the man that was most likely David yelled, rushing into the sitting room from one of the closed doors, which she assumed was a bedroom. He brandished an axe and swung it wildly.

The thing that struck Delia as peculiar was the bandage over one of his eyes.

"David?" Delia questioned, since she had never met him and wasn't sure what he looked like. She couldn't find any trace of him online when she tried looking on the flight to Asheville.

David stopped and looked at her, then at Carter. "Who are you and why are you in my house? You're trespassing on private property!"

Delia raised her hands in a gesture of peace. "I'm Delia and this is my partner, Carter. We're private investigators working on the case involving Edgar Peterson. We were trying to track him down and bring him back to the prison. Are you his friend?"

David glared at Delia. "It doesn't matter who I am because he's dead, so you can't bring him anywhere."

"How did he die?" Delia asked, gulping and trying to hide her fear. Was David as psychotic as Edgar was? What were they dealing with now?

"I killed him," David said simply, gripping the axe tightly in his hand. "And now I'm going to kill both of you."

But David didn't have a chance to use his axe on them because the second he lunged at Delia, she fired her gun, hitting David in the chest. Her decade of experience on the police force had trained her for this type of situation. David screamed as the bullet hit him, then stumbled from the force, dropping the axe, and falling to the ground.

Delia calmly walked over to David. His blood was spilling out from his chest wound and soaking the wooden floor. David clutched his chest, moaning in pain. With his other hand, he felt around the floor, presumably trying to find his axe. Delia kicked the axe out of his reach. She didn't want to take any chances.

"Call 911," Delia said to Carter.

Carter hastily dialed 911 and talked to a dispatcher, who told them it would be at least a half hour before anyone could reach the cabin, since it was in the middle of the woods and there wasn't a hospital nearby.

Delia looked at Carter anxiously when he hung up the phone. "He's going to die."

Carter solemnly looked at David, bleeding out on the roughly hewn wooden floor. "Well, the bastard deserves what's coming for him. He was going to hurt you."

Delia's heart raced at Carter's words, but she told herself he only said that because they were partners. She was his boss and they had become friends since they started working together. Being thrown into situations involving dangerous criminals like kidnappers and serial killers tended to make people bond in a way like nothing else did. That was it. In the short amount of time they had known each other, they almost died multiple times, so of course they were close.

"Thanks for acting so quickly. He had a crazy look in his eyes and I don't think he could have been reasoned with. But I froze up when I saw him come for you. I'm sorry."

"It's fine," Delia said, nearly collapsing as her legs became inexplicably weak.

Carter rushed to her side. "Are you okay?"

"Yeah, I'm fine. Just a bit overwhelmed. It happened so fast."

"You sure?"

"Yeah. And this may not be the best time to say it, but I want to hire you to work for my company full-time."

Carter grinned. "I would love to."

Chapter 42: Delia

Delia was back at home in Becca and Joel's house. Becca and Joel were out on their first date in months, so she was home alone with Lily and enjoying the first peaceful night to herself in what felt like forever. She filled the bathtub with bubble bath, lit a few candles, and soaked in the tub for a relaxing half hour. Afterwards, she dried off and put on her comfiest lounge clothes, preparing herself for a night of wine, chocolate, and watching a dumb movie on Netflix that she didn't have to pay attention to.

As she endlessly scrolled through Netflix and tried to find a movie, the doorbell rang, and startled her. She hadn't expected anyone. Lily barked her head off at whoever was at the door. She stiffened. Who could it be? She checked the time. Becca and Joel shouldn't be home for at least a few more hours and they had keys to the house, so they wouldn't ring the doorbell. She stood to peek through the window and saw Carter standing on the doorstep. Shit.

She was wearing a ratty, stained, old T-shirt and joggers. Her hair was wet from the bath and her face was free of make-up. She shook her head. Did it matter? It was only Carter.

She answered the door. "Carter, I wasn't expecting to see you until Monday."

Carter paused before he replied when he noticed she wore what appeared to be pajamas and had apparently just taken a bath or shower. "Ah, sorry for dropping by like this." His face flushed in embarrassment. "I should have called first and made sure you didn't have plans."

"It's fine. Why did you stop by?" she asked, casually leaning against the doorframe.

"I brought dinner. I thought we could hang out tonight," he replied, holding up a bag of takeout food.

Delia's stomach grumbled and she realized she never ate dinner.

"I can leave if you don't feel like hanging out," Carter said after Delia remained silent and didn't invite him inside.

"No, I'm hungry, trust me. Come inside," she said, opening the door all the way so he could enter the house.

Carter smiled brightly and walked straight into the kitchen, pulling out plates and silverware from the cupboards and dishing up food for both of them, making himself right at home. He seated himself beside Delia on the couch and glanced at the TV.

"So, what are we watching?" he asked, as he shoved a large portion of food into his mouth.

Delia hesitated. She planned to watch a romcom or some other sort of cheesy movie while she spent the night at home alone, but now that Carter was here—

"For the record, I love a good romcom almost as much as a compelling mystery," Carter said with a wicked grin, as he gestured at the movie Delia had paused on her browsing through Netflix.

Delia grinned back and hit play on the movie.

Acknowledgements

I have so many people to thank. So many people who were a part of helping me bring my first book series to life.

First, my wonderful, wonderful husband, Zed. He's the one who painstakingly formatted each of my books. He's also supported me since the very beginning, even before I published my first book. He encouraged me to finally finish The Long Shadow on the Stage. He dealt with me spending countless nights writing, editing, marketing, researching self-publishing, and endlessly talking about book-related things. He's the one who sets up my vendor booth and tent at every in-person event I attend and sits by my side all day for moral support. I couldn't do any of this without his unwavering support and love.

Mandi Lynn, who owns Stone Ridge Books, is the one who designed all three of my beautiful book covers. She's been so great to work with and has helped me bring my visions to life with her artistic talent.

My amazing beta readers. Zedekiah Heydenburg, Kate Postma, Alex Noelke Robert Hayek, Ren Skinner, and Michele Packard. Your valuable feedback helped me shape this book series, made the characters more believable, and assisted with solving plot holes.

Special shout-out to a few Bookstagrammers/book reviewers/ARC readers who read my books, wrote reviews, and helped more readers find *The Long Shadow* series. @becca_loves_reading.

@onnikkisbookshelf.

@amysbookshelfreviews.

@bookshelf_adventures, and many others.

Thank you also to all my awesome writing friends I have made over the past few years! I wouldn't be able to get through the struggles, share in my successes, and continue writing without you. Robert Hayek, Michele Packard, L.C. McKenna, Alyssa Green, Jamie Lee Fry, and others.

And last but not least, to you, my readers. The ones who have been there since the beginning. The ones who anxiously awaited the final book in the trilogy. The ones who messaged me, emailed me, or commented on my posts asking when the next book was coming out. The ones who posted a book review, shared my social media posts, told your friends and family about my books, and helped spread the word that my books are worth the read. The ones who just discovered my books. All of you. Thank you.

Note from the Author

If you want to help me, I would appreciate it immensely if you wrote an honest review for *The Long Shadow of Death*. Posting your review online is one of the best ways to support indie authors. Reviews help other readers decide which books they want to buy and allow indie authors to gain more exposure to new readers. Please consider posting an honest review on the book retailer website where you purchased the book and/or on Goodreads.

Subscribe

If you're interested in being a part of the first group of readers to learn about:

- My upcoming book releases and works in progress.
- Exclusive book content.
- Book sales and freebies.
- Giveaways.
- Notifications when I'm having a book signing.

Sign up for my newsletter on www.nicholeheydenburg.com!

www.ingramcontent.com/pod-product-compliance
Lightning Source LLC
Chambersburg PA
CBHW061616190726
48288CB00007B/2352